3 9078 00126670 0

DISCARD

THE HOWARD HUGHES AFFAIR

Reedsburg Public Library
345 Vine St.
Reedsburg, Wi. 53959

THE HOWARD HUGHES AFFAIR

by

STUART M. KAMINSKY

ST. MARTIN'S PRESS • NEW YORK

Copyright © 1979 by Stuart M. Kaminsky
All rights reserved. For information, write:
St. Martin's Press, Inc., 175 Fifth Ave., New York, N.Y. 10010.
Manufactured in the United States of America

Library of Congress Cataloging in Publication Data

Kaminsky, Stuart M.
The Howard Hughes affair.

1. Hughes, Howard Robard, 1905-1976—Fiction.
I. Title.
PZ4.K1497Ho [PS3561.A43] 813'.5'4 79-5032
ISBN 0-312-39617-1

"We have got to the deductions and the inferences," said Lestrade, winking at me. "I find it hard enough to tackle facts, Holmes, without flying away after theories and fancies."

"You are right," said Holmes demurely; "you do find it very hard to tackle the facts."

—*The Boscombe Valley Mystery,*
Sir Arthur Conan Doyle

THE HOWARD HUGHES AFFAIR

CHAPTER ONE

The microphone and boom thudded down on the stage within a sigh of taking off the toes of my bare right foot. I had taken the shoe off because the bottom of my right foot began to itch after an hour of waiting in the dark studio at NBC. With the microphone still rolling into the wings, I reached for my shoe and sock, went flat on my stomach and squinted into the darkness.

Things were not going right for me. I had conned my way past the night guard and taken a seat on the side of the stage where I could see anyone who came into Studio B. The killer was supposed to wait for me to contact my informant before making his move—and getting caught. It was all very reasonable and simple, but the killer didn't seem to understand what was expected of him.

The dim corridor light behind the killer caught a glint of metal in the audience. Studio B was soundproof. I could be dead without anyone knowing it till morning. At 44, I was still agile and ugly, but with one shoe off and against a pistol I was too slow and unarmed. In addition to which there wasn't a hell of a lot of room to hide. Even if I could get to my .38, which I had left in the glove compartment of my car, I had never shot a human in my life in spite of seven years as a Glendale cop, five more as a Warner Brothers security guard and almost five years as a private investigator. In stark contrast, my friend in the audience had done away with three people in the last five days. I was seriously outclassed.

At any time except two in the morning, someone would pass the studio and look in—an announcer, a producer, somebody—but I had done too good a job of setting myself up.

The killer stepped forward carefully, showing first the barrel of his gun and then his silhouette clearly against the dim light from the hall. When the shot came, I rolled hard toward the control booth at the back of the stage, abandoning my shoe in mid-air and throwing a kick at the door. The shot didn't have the sharp crack I knew and hated. It had a muffled sound like a gorilla spitting. Any sane man given the choice of kicking a door with a shoe-covered foot or bare one would have chosen the shoe-covered foot, but Toby Peters was not a sane man. He was a cornered, one-shoed idiot who had thought he had a plan to catch a killer and instead wound up victim Number Four—maybe.

In spite of a bad back, very few friends, and a small bank account, I had one hell of an impulse toward self-preservation. I rolled into the control booth on my side and scrambled over a chair until I came against the wall under the main panel. I could hear the stage boards creak slightly as the killer followed. His grey shadow played against the back wall and scared the hell out of me. I clenched my teeth and tried to salivate to keep from gagging and giving myself away. My foot was sore from kicking the door and so was I. I had been warned by my client not to do this, but why should I take advice from Howard Hughes on how to catch a killer? Did I tell him how to invest a million, design an airplane, direct a movie? The killer with the silencer, meanwhile, was making his way toward the control booth door I had left open.

I inched my way out from under the panel toward the far end of the booth, trying to remember if there was a door there. I got to my knees slowly, and crawled to the wall. There was a door. The footsteps were no more than fifteen feet away, and if I turned, I was sure I'd find myself looking into the barrel of the pistol and its too quiet death. I grabbed for the door, missed, grabbed again and ran like hell in hope that the killer's aim would stay sour. A second shot tore into the acoustical wall on my right. I pulled off my shoe on the run and threw it over my shoulder in the general direction of the booth in the brilliant hope that it would slow him down. There were no running footsteps behind me, and I prayed to gods unknown that the killer was willing to call it a day if I was.

I got to the studio door and limped toward the front lobby.

I limped not because I was shoeless but because one foot hurt from kicking the door, and the other had stepped on something sharp in the darkness. There was a swinging door just before the lobby, and I plunged through it looking for help. The night receptionist wasn't there. Neither was the night guard. I hobbled toward the front door. No one was on the street so I dragged my foot around the corner to the parking lot where I made my painful way to my rusting green Buick sitting like a sad turtle, catching the light of the moon on its dirty windshield. I got in, retrieved my .38 from the glove compartment, put it on the dashboard, took a quick look toward the NBC building to see no one there and yanked out my keys. The Buick turned over but jerked forward, banging my head into the steering wheel and sending the .38 and a half-used box of Kleenex flying into the back seat. One of my tires was flat. I turned around to scramble for the .38 in the shadows, missed it and caught a glimpse of a figure with a gun walking slowly across the lot toward me. Bullet Number Three turned my front windshield into a spider web. It was a fascinating pattern, but I didn't have time to admire it or wonder where the hell the population of Los Angeles was. I pushed the door open after one more frantic search for the pistol and rolled onto the gravel.

My grey zipper gabardine windbreaker from Muller and Bluett's was holding up reasonably well, but my expenses were mounting—a flat tire, cracked windshield, medication and treatment for a lacerated foot. I got to my knees and scrambled around a couple of cars toward the side of the NBC building, counting my assets.

These included about 17 years of dubious experience and darkness to hide me. On the debit side, I thought as I stumbled toward what looked like a door, I had a bum foot, no pistol, no help and a calm killer behind me. I hit the side door hard, expecting to bounce off it like a bullet against steel, but it gave and I tumbled back into NBC.

Gary Cooper had probably been in this carpeted corridor once, but where was he when I needed him? I wondered what he would have done in my place. I knew he would have had both shoes on and a gun in his hand. I was getting closer and closer to the point of imagining how the discovery of my body would look. I wanted to be at least a semidignified corpse. I could see my brother Phil the cop standing over me, looking down at my bruised bare feet and thinking it was just the kind of nonsense he expected. Maybe he'd spend a few days trying to figure out why the killer had taken me to NBC, removed my shoes and tortured me before putting me away. The prospect gave me as much incentive to keep moving as did the likelihood of my death.

Footsteps trampled gravel outside the door I had just dived through. The long barrel of the pistol came into view, and I scrambled down the hall smelling the carpet, the walls, and people. I was aware of too much. It was a sure sign of fear.

In the second or two it took the character with the gun to step into the light, I pushed at a door. It didn't give. Bullet Number Four missed.

A plan came to mind while I panted and ran. It was just as bad as my other plans: I decided to scream until someone in the damn building heard me. The hell with dignity. I'd even take an old cleaning lady. But I changed my mind. What difference would a cleaning lady or two make to someone who was out to equal the record of Billy the Kid?

I wondered if the guy with the gun had noticed that I wasn't shooting back. I thought about trying to get back to the door and my Buick, find that damn .38 and hide in the hope the killer would give up and go to breakfast or the toilet. My foot told me I'd never make it.

A light came up on my right and I looked into a soundproof studio where a guy with earphones was sitting and talking into a microphone. He had one hand on his forehead and was reading from a sheet in front of him.

I pounded on the window but he didn't hear me, which may have been just as well for him. Behind him in a small booth was a dozing engineer. I pushed my face against the glass and pounded harder on the window. The engineer looked up at my flattened visage, rubbed his mouth with his open palm and reached for his glasses, but a sound behind me told me I had no time to wait. I turned a corridor, sure I was leaving a trail of blood from my increasingly painful foot in NBC's clean blue carpet, and pushed through the first door that would open. I fell flat, landing on a table piled with records. The table cracked and records went rolling and flying. My breath was gone. I pushed myself to my knees, wiped sweat from my eyes and listened. No footsteps, just the distant sound of Tommy Dorsey playing "This Love of Mine."

I reached over to close the door behind me, gasping for air. I was in a small record storage room. With the slight light from under the door, I could see that there was only one way in or out of the room. Then a shadow appeared under the door. Someone was standing on the other side.

I was scared and angry—angry because anyone in his right mind would have given odds that the destruction of NBC would have brought an army of guards swooping down even at two in the morning. Anger didn't keep fear from turning my stomach. I reached back and felt my way around a large cabinet. It opened with almost no noise and I found enough room inside even with the stacks of records to climb in and close the door behind me. The door wouldn't stay shut, but by holding onto the sharp end of a corroded nail that stuck through the wood, I was able to keep it closed. I knew my fingers would cramp eventually, and I would have been more comfortable in a position other than on my back with my throbbing foot in the air and the Andrews Sisters' version of "Elmer's Tune" poking my neck, but I was alive and had hope.

The door to the small room opened and I heard a foot crunch against one of the records I had scattered. Footsteps on more records, and the light came on in the room and filtered through the cracks in the cabinet.

The footsteps made it clear that the killer was no more than the length of a tall man away. The length dwindled to midget height with one step and there was a tug at the cabinet door. I held onto my rusty nail as tightly as I could, folded upside down on my back. The cabinet door opened and the light hit my face.

My hope that some of the noise had penetrated the brain of a curious guard fell away when I saw the long pistol. I tumbled out of my tiny tomb as the killer stepped back and levelled the gun at me. There was no great hurry now. I put my back against the wall and stood up to take the shot. My knees were too cramped and weak to even consider a lunge. I shrugged and looked up at the face behind the rifle. It was a familiar face, the face of someone who had killed at least two people. The barrel of the gun came up and I revised the body count upward by one.

CHAPTER TWO

It had all started six days earlier. Actually, where it started is a question of what you're interested in. It started for me in about March of 1897 when my father and mother decided to have a second offspring and God provided a convenient rainstorm one afternoon, so they could close their grocery and work on it. Nine months later on November 14, Tobias Leo Pevsner, who was to become Toby Peters, detective and shoeless victim, was born. Jump 44 years, a broken nose, a broken marriage, and as many broken promises as there are abandoned wrecks along the Pacific Coast Highway and you find yourself in my rooming house, on a Monday, one week before my showdown at NBC.

On the Friday before, I had called a number given to me by my ex-wife Anne, who worked for Transcontinental and World Airlines. According to Anne, her boss's boss, Howard Hughes, wanted a good, honest detective. I qualified for at least the second half of that requirement. I had called the number and spent the weekend at the library getting information on Hughes. He had broken all sorts of long distance flying records, owned Hughes Aircraft in Culver City, Hughes Tool Company, a good chunk of Transcontinental, the Caddo Corporation for making movies, a brewery in Texas and large parts of six states. I was impressed, primarily because I figured it would be reasonable to ask a guy like Hughes for $50 a day, which was so far out of line that anyone but a millionaire would have laughed at it.

On Monday morning, I was sitting in my room eating a very large bowl of Kellogg's All-Bran, the natural laxative cereal. I had been living in a rooming house in Hollywood for almost three months at $15 a month.

I had no faith in the rooming house lasting a long time. My last place was being levelled by a bulldozer to make way for a supermarket. I had been thrown out of the apartment I had lived in before that when a guy shot it up and took an unintended dive out of my window. The rooming house was a change of pace in a quiet neighborhood. It had been an impulsive move toward domestic tranquility, but the quiet street and deaf landlady were already driving me away from what little sanity I had.

The deaf landlady, Mrs. Plaut, kept the room clean, which relieved me of the small, infrequent guilt I had always felt about the other places I had lived in and let rot around me. I had a hot plate in a corner, a sink, a small refrigerator, some dishes, a table and three chairs, a rug, a bed with a purple blanket made by Mrs. Plaut that said ''God Bless Us Every One'' in pink stitching, and a sofa with little doilies on the arms that I was afraid to touch.

The six people who lived in the place generally minded their own business. I wasn't even sure who they all were, since my hours were unusual and I didn't socialize much in the hall or join in the weekly poker game Mrs. Plaut held in the living room downstairs. Eventually, I would have to accept her invitation since she assured me the stakes were "moderate." I had trouble picturing her wrapped in her old shawl crocheting doilies as she "raised a sawbuck" over the eleven-cent bet of Mr. Hill, the nearsighted accountant.

The phone in the hall rang and I could hear Mrs. Plaut cackling to someone. Then I heard the slap of her slippered feet come down the hall. I could almost smell the faded flowers on her print dress when she knocked on my door.

"Tony," she whispered. I had spent the better part of the first evening I moved in trying to tell her my name was Toby, but she had smiled knowingly and kept calling me Tony Peelers. I had enough names and could have done without it, but some things aren't worth the effort.

"O.K.," I shouted, shoveling down All-Bran so it wouldn't get soggy while I went to the phone.

"Tony," she went on. "Are you there? You have a telephone call."

"I'm here. I'll be right there."

Her feet padded away, and I hurried to the door, pulling on my pants. I hobbled down the corridor to hear Mrs. Plaut saying into the phone, "I'm sorry, but Tony is not home. Would you care to leave a message?"

I managed to pull my belt tight and wave to Mrs. Plaut, who ignored me. We wrestled for the phone for a few seconds. Since I was thirty years younger than she was and fifty pounds heavier, I almost succeeded in getting the phone from her fingers. I finally forced my face in front of her, and recognition dawned. She let me have the phone and I panted into it.

"Peters here."

"Mr. Hughes would like to see you today," a male voice said.

"All right, where?"

"Be at 7000 Romaine at 11. That gives you one hour."

"One hour," I said. "What's it about?"

The guy on the other end hung up and so did I.

I finished my cereal, had another bowl with sugar and milk and found out from the L.A. *Times* that the Russians had launched a strong counteroffensive against the Nazis at Rostov, that Rommel was holding the British in Libya, and that F.D.R. saw a crisis in Asia while he waited for the Japanese reply to his principles for peace. "War Clouds Loom in the Pacific," said the headlines. I turned to the sports section and found that Hugh Gallarnea, the former Stanford runner, had led the World Championship Chicago Bears to a 49–14 win over the Philadelphia Eagles with three touchdowns. Green Bay was still a game ahead of Chicago in the Western Division with a 10–1 record compared to Chicago's 9–1. I had developed a strong curiousity about Chicago since a recent visit there, and I wondered how anyone could play, or want to play football in a Chicago winter.

I also discovered from the "Private Lives" cartoon that "Berlin's most luxurious boudoir belongs, not to a movie star, but to Reinhard Heydrich the cold-blooded killer who governs what was once Czecho-Slovakia."

Armed with all this information, I shaved, finished dressing, rinsed out my bowl, pretended I didn't notice my unmade bed and went into the rain ignoring the twinge in my bad back that promised trouble if the rain kept up.

Three little girls about eight years old were skipping rope on the porch. I watched them for awhile, waiting for a break in the rain so I could dash to the Buick, tilt my hat back and feel like a detective.

The girl who was jumping had three teeth missing on top, and her mouth was wide open. The two rope-turners chanted:

> Fudge, fudge, tell the judge
> Mother has a newborn baby;
> It isn't a girl and it isn't a boy;
> It's just a fair young lady.
> Wrap it up in tissue paper
> And send it up the elevator;
> First floor, miss;
> Second floor, miss;
> Third floor, miss;
> Fourth floor,
> Kick it out the elevator door.

Since that was about all I could take from the youth of America on two bowls of All-Bran, I dashed for the car and made it without too much rain damage to my suit.

Seven thousand Romaine was a big office building, and they were expecting me. A young man who looked like an ex-seminary student with his blond hair parted almost down the middle identified himself as Dean and escorted me up the elevator, commenting on the weather, the misfortunes of war, and our mutual hope for prosperity. I said he was right and followed him past a maze of rooms. Everyone seemed to have been set down in isolated cubbyholes.

Dean read my mind and kept walking.

"Mr. Hughes prefers to keep the employees separated so they won't gossip and they won't know what each is doing. He believes in keeping company secrets."

We went into a large office with a thick, blue carpet and pictures of birds on the wall. There was a bar, table, radio, desk and a hell of a good view. But it looked unused.

The young guy read my mind again, which was probably what he got paid for.

"This office is for Mr. Hughes, but he never comes here."

"Today is special."

He nodded his head negatively.

"No, today is not special. You are to wait here for a call from Mr. Hughes."

"Life's been threatened and he's being careful," I guessed, taking a walk to the window.

"No," said the man, his mouth playing with the idea of being amused. "This is Mr. Hughes' normal procedure."

"I see," I said knowingly.

Dean checked the unused desk to be sure it was neat. "I don't know why he does two-thirds of what he does. And I don't know why he wants to see you."

"Terrific," I said, turning to smile at him, knowing that my smile made me look like an enraptured gargoyle.

We stared at each other for half an hour and looked at the phone. At noon, a tray of food came in. According to Dean, Hughes himself had ordered my lunch, which turned out to be a salad, a bacon and avocado sandwich on white bread and a big glass of milk. Dean had the same. We ate in silence at a small table, and I felt my mind toying with catatonia.

"Can I get you anything more?" he said when he finished and wiped his mouth with a napkin. "More food? Something to drink or read?"

"How about another avocado sandwich to go?" I tried. He didn't look angry or amused. We waited some more and I looked at my watch. It told me it was 12:45, which might be true or might be hours off.

I turned on the radio without permission, tuned in KFI and listened to *Vic and Sade*. Uncle Fletcher and Sade spent the show talking about how they were going to have lunch together. When it was over, a buzzer on the desk jerked young Dean forward. He grabbed the phone, said "yes," and hung up.

"There's a private airport in Burbank on. . ." Dean started.

"I know where it is," I cut in.

"Good. You're to go there immediately."

"What if I don't go there immediately? What if I don't like being treated like a vacuum-cleaner salesman?"

"Sorry?" said Dean as if he hadn't heard me.

"What if I don't feel like going to Burbank? What if I decide instead to invest 30 cents and see *Citizen Kane* at the Hawaiian instead, and maybe another 40 cents on a couple of tacos?"

"It would probably cost me my job," he said.

"It doesn't seem like much of a goddamn job to me, Dean," I said, making for the door.

"Mr. Dean, Walter Dean," he corrected. "It pays

well,'' he said with a sign of life, ''and you get to meet all kinds of strange people.''

''Like Howard Hughes?''

''Believe it or not, Mr. Peters, you and I have already had a longer conversation than any I have had with Mr. Hughes. I hope you enjoy *Citizen Kane*.''

I looked at him and couldn't tell if he meant it or the whole response was some kind of con to keep me in a good mood. If he was a fake, he was a good one.

''Burbank?'' I said.

He nodded and I left, hurrying down the silent, carpeted corridors and out of the damn building as fast as I could. My footsteps didn't even echo to keep me company. The building had no echo. And there were no people walking down the halls chatting and no people at the water coolers. There were no water coolers.

I was already in love with Howard Hughes as I drove to Burbank in the rain listening to *Young Widder Brown*. I stopped at a drug store for a Coke after the radio told me, ''A little minute for a big rest means more and better work.'' It was sound advice, and though I was normally addicted to Pepsi, I proved my flexibility. I also bought a tube of Musterole salve to use on my back when I got home. If it was good enough for the Dionne Quintuplets, and the radio said it was, then it was good enough for Toby Peters. I tried to think of a scheme for getting Carmen, the widow cashier at Levy's Grill, to invite me to her place for a Musterole treatment. I'd even invest 30 cents and take her with me to the Hawaiian. With more than 300 dollars in the bank and a potential millionaire client coming up, I could afford a few luxuries, maybe even a full tank of gas.

The rain had turned to steady sheets of thin, sticky glue by the time I hit the airport. I parked in a small lot and ran for the nearest building. Two guys stopped me before I hit the safety of the tin overhang. Both were well dressed, unsmiling and dry. They were also big. At least one of them should have been ugly, but they weren't. They looked like everyone's image of the FBI.

"I'm supposed to meet Hughes here," I said, holding my hand over my head to keep a small patch of my scalp dry.

They parted to let me by.

"Thanks," I said, dripping between them and through a white, wooden door. They followed me in, looking confident. I didn't like it, and I didn't like meeting a potential client wearing a seersucker sponge.

"You should have asked me for my name," I said, looking around the small, empty office.

One of the grey pair of movie doubles stepped forward and I turned, expecting trouble and maybe wanting it. The wait in Hughes' office and the game in the rain had made me tough and stupid. The grey double handed me a card. On the card was my photograph. I nodded, handed it back, and sat down at a bench across from an old desk covered with bills and paper. The rain pinged in boredom on the tin roof as one of the two went back outside and the other stayed to keep his eyes on me.

"What now?" I asked. "Do I get blindfolded and transported to Northern Canada?"

"Mr. Hughes will be right down," he said. He and Walter Dean back on Romaine had gone to the same school. I could hear the buzzing of a small airplane outside and turned to look across the field. A dot appeared in the distance out of the waves of dark rain and grew larger as it headed toward us and touched down on the ground with a slight bump and whirr. The plane, a two-engine silver thing, kept getting bigger and moving slower till it came to a stop about thirty yards from us. Two men climbed out, one well built and wearing a light-colored suit, the other tall and thin with slacks and an old zipper jacket. The one in the suit ran ahead while the thin guy ambled, ignoring the rain and deep in thought. The guy in the suit burst through the door, panting. He was about fifty with thick glasses. He looked at me, took off his jacket, snapped it once to get the top layer of moisture off and looked at the door. The second man came in. He pushed back his wet, dark hair and clenched his teeth without looking at anyone and unzipped his battered jacket, revealing a clean white shirt and no tie. Something was on his mind. He was in his mid-thirties, about six-foot four and had a slight mustache, which couldn't make up its mind whether to be something admirable or something inconspicuous. From the way the business-suited duo looked at him trying not to look at him, I assumed he was Hughes.

"Noah, tell Rod to back it another eighth of a revolution. No, make it a seventh. I'll take it up as soon as it's done." The guy who had been in the plane with Hughes nodded, put his wet jacket back on and went into the rain without a word. Hughes sat at the edge of the desk, looking out of the window at the resting plane. He touched his lower lip, looked through me, and closed his eyes. Inspiration hit, and he turned to pick up the phone.

"Did Noah get there yet, Rod?" he shouted, as if unsure of the power of the phone to carry his voice.

"Right, well in addition to the seventh, check the rear flaps again. I know you did." Hughes hung up and crossed his arms. I gave him about three more minutes while I tried to gain sympathy from the guy who looked like the FBI, but he wasn't having any.

Finally, I said, "Mr. Hughes."

Hughes didn't answer, and I got up. This time I was a little louder.

"Mr. Hughes."

Nothing.

The third time, I gave it something close to a shout. Hughes looked up.

He turned his eyes on me and slowly focused into the room.

"You're. . ."

"Peters, Toby Peters. I eat avocado and bacon sandwiches, wait around in blue offices for hours, take long rides in the rain, and occasionally do a confidential investivation."

Hughes looked at me with serious interest for the first time.

"You're five-foot nine, 44 years old. Your brother is an LAPD police lieutenant in the Wilshire District. You have an office in the Farraday Building, exactly $323 in the bank and a bad back which must be causing you some pain now because it flares up in humid weather."

"What kind of gun do I have?"

He paused for a second, chewed on his mustache with his lower teeth, cocked his head as if he hadn't heard. Apparently he was a little hard of hearing and didn't feel like admitting it, so I asked the question louder.

"You own a .38 automatic, but you've never fired it

at anyone and you don't like to carry it. You have a good record with a reputation for knowing how to keep secrets. That's important to me."

"Thanks," I said.

"You also have a reputation for doing foolish things."

He did something that looked as if it might someday develop into a smile. Then his head twitched slightly in the direction of the door. It was enough of a message to send his well-dressed muscle man back out into the rain, closing the door behind him.

Hughes, his arms still folded across his chest and his rear against the desk, turned his eyes upward, looking at the ceiling and listening to the rain hit the roof.

"This country is going to be at war in a few weeks," he said.

It seemed both reasonable and inevitable to me, and I had nothing to add. In a few minutes, he went on.

"Hughes Aircraft has designed some important equipment to help us win that war. We have finished plans for the D-2 bomber, the fastest, most accurate bomber plane in the world. We have also completed designs for a long-range, high-speed, giant wooden transport for carrying troops to Europe over the Atlantic or Pacific to bypass the threat of submarines."

"Sounds great," I said, waiting for him to tell me if I was going to pilot the bomber or the transport.

"I have reason to believe the Japanese have either stolen my plans or have tried to steal them." He turned his eyes on me. They didn't blink. I looked back at him, wondering what the hell my reaction was supposed to be. I nodded slowly, sadly, knowingly. It was a good choice. He went on.

"In 1934, we built the H-1, the Hughes One, a prototype for the world's fastest landplane. It had a radial engine with two banks of cylinders and a 1,000-horsepower Pratt and Whitney twin Wasp engine."

I raised my eyebrows in further appreciation though I didn't know a Pratt and Whitney from a gumball machine. Hughes was looking straight at me and talking.

"We built that to run fast, even specified flathead screws countersunk and rivets installed flush with the metal to minimize wind resistance. We set a world speed record in that plane in 1935 in Santa Anna. Now the Japanese have a fighter plane they're using in China, based on the H-1, and the United States is a good five years behind them."

"Mr. Hughes," I said, getting up and trying not to reach for my aching back, "I don't know a damn thing about airplanes."

"But you know a lot about thieves," he said.

"I've caught them, lost them, played poker with them and been laid up by them. They come in all sizes and ages: old ladies in grocery stores who drop cans of soup in their knitting bags; fourteen-year-olds who break pawnshop windows to grab watches they can't sell; guys with guns and no brains and guys with enough brains to be making ten times as much in something straight. I even know guys who own big companies who might qualify, and I don't mean you. I want a hot bath and you want the cops or the FBI, not me."

Hughes moved away from the desk toward me. A bead of water dripped down his forehead, and he looked tired as he stepped forward.

"The FBI doesn't believe me, and the police who have jurisdiction can't handle it."

"Right," I said, looking at him after a step toward the door. "What could I do? Play spy? Break codes?"

"You could listen," he said, showing a distinct spark of irritation. He tried to cover it like an exposed sore, and the look in his eyes was embarrassment.

"I don't get together with people very much," he said carefully. "But last Monday I had a small dinner for some people who I thought might be of value when the war came. My plan was to organize a kind of lobby to support the projects I think are vital if we are to win that war. We're already gearing up to munitions work and. . ." he trailed off, making it clear there were things I didn't have to know. I agreed with him. There was a lot I didn't have to know. My specialty was guarding bodies and hotel lobbies, finding runaway wives, husbands, parents and kids, lovers and deadbeats—not spies.

"Hear me out, Peters," he said with a tone of anger, as my face showed my decision. He was about to say something else when the telephone rang. We looked into each others' eyes while he talked loudly on the phone, "Right, yes, I'll be right there. No, I'll do it." He hung up and gritted his teeth.

"Peters, I want you to quietly investigate the list of people I am going to give you. They were dinner guests last week at the house I'm using in Mirador down near Laguna. I also have the names of the three servants who were there. I'm sure someone on the night of that dinner went into the study and looked at my plans for the bomber and the transport. My papers were moved. I want you to find out who looked at those papers and if they actually got to copy them."

I shook my head sadly. He looked at his watch.

"Look," I said, "You can get a whole agency to work on this. Besides, I don't think I can come up with anything based on what you've got. You've got maybes and you want miracles."

Hughes moved toward the door and past me.

"You were recommended by one of our employees. You check out. No one can buy you off and no one can make you talk. I'll give you $48 a day plus expenses. Walter Dean at the Romaine Office will be your contact and give you anything you need. Now, it's either yes or no. I've got to get back on the field."

If he was waiting for me to ask how he came up with a figure like $48, he was going to be disappointed, but he was also a man who knew the price of another man.

"No guarantees and $100 in advance," I said.

"Ninety-six dollars in advance, two days," he said.

I laughed and he considered the matter ended because he pulled a neatly folded sheet of paper from his pocket and handed it to me.

On the sheet were typed the names, phone numbers, home and business addresses of nine people, along with the reasons for their being invited to the Hughes dinner.

I started to say something, but Hughes shook his head no.

"You don't like me, do you, Peters?" he said with his hand on the doorknob.

"—I like your money," I said.

"My father died when I was a kid," Hughes said. "He was a tough man, but a man everybody liked. My father knew how to laugh. He was a terrifically loved man. I am not. I don't have the ability to win people the way he did. I have no interest in studying people. I should be more interested in people, but I can't. I am interested in science, in nature, the earth. I can work with that. That's why I need people like you, people who are used to working with emotions and lies. If you have to reach me, reach me through Dean." He turned and left.

The man called Noah came in almost passing Hughes at the door. Without a word, Noah took out a thick wallet, handed me $96 in various bills and made out a receipt for me to sign.

"We'll want an itemized bill," he said.

"That's what I always give," I said.

"We know," he said. "I think he respects you, Peters."

I shrugged.

"I'm grateful," I said, counting the money and putting it into my own nearly empty wallet.

"He doesn't want gratitude," Noah said, moving to the window to watch Hughes take off into the rain. "I don't know what the hell he wants. Do you know how many times he's had that plane up today in this rain? Thirty-five times. He's convinced there's something wrong with it that no one else can find. He's been up for three straight days and nights working on it and he'll be up and in the air till he's satisfied."

"A perfectionist," I sighed, starting to shiver from being wet.

"No," sighed Noah. "It's more like a disease. It itches

at him, drives him mad like a song you can't remember or a name on the tip of your tongue."

"You're a philosopher, like Irving Berlin," I said, moving to the door.

"No," he said, "a wet, glorified bookkeeper."

On the way out, I nodded to bodyguards one and two and dashed through the rain to my Buick. Hughes had taken off over me and was disappearing into a bank of dark clouds.

In the Buick, I let out my first groan of the last hour and rubbed the spot far back above my kidney where the pain was worst. Experience told me if I didn't get out of these wet clothes and stand up or lie flat on the floor within the next half hour, I might not be able to walk for days, but I couldn't resist a quick look at the list Hughes had given me. I wiped the pain from my brow and pulled the sheet out. The neat list included Basil Rathbone, actor; Anton Gurstwald, chairman of Farbentek of America; his wife, Trudi Gurstwald; Ernest Barton, Major, Army Air Corps.; Norma Forney, writer; Benjamin Siegel, businessman; Toshiro Homoto, houseboy–chauffeur; Martin Schell, cook; William Nuss, butler. All telephone-listed, all addressed, all ready to be investigated, though I didn't expect to come up with anything except an improved bank account.

CHAPTER THREE

I drove back to Hollywood, my rooming house and a shower. The hot water smacked me low on the back for about fifteen minutes while I blew air out of my almost flat nostrils to prove I could still do it. Then I put on a pair of shorts and a T-shirt and got my back on the faded carpet in my room to stare at the ceiling and wait for the pain to pass.

It was so peaceful I almost fell asleep. After ten minutes, Gunther Wherthman, who had the room next to mine and who had convinced Mrs. Plaut to take me in in spite of my profession, dropped by to keep me company. His visit was formal, as always, and he was too polite to comment on my prone position. So I explained. Our eyes were in reasonable contact, and I didn't have to raise my voice. Gunther is a midget. We had met when I blundered into the solution to a murder he was accused of. We had been something like friends ever since, ever since being less than a year. Gunther was Swiss, but was usually taken for German, which caused him some difficulty since Germans were not particularly popular in the States in 1941. Since he was a small possible-German, he was especially vulnerable.

Gunther always wore a neat suit and spent most of his time in his room translating books and articles from German, French, Italian, Spanish and Polish into English. Sometimes it paid reasonably well. Usually it was about as lucrative as being a private detective. Gunther didn't like to talk. I loved talking. We got along great. If someone had burst in on us, we would have looked something like a tableau from a wax museum, me as the corpse on the floor, he as the tiny killer pondering his crime. As it was, Mrs. Plaut did stick her head in, looking for something or someone. Our positions either did not register with her or seventy years of living in Hollywood had prepared her for anything.

"I've got a client," I told Gunther.

"As have I," he said.

We were quiet for another ten minutes.

"I'm supposed to find some spies," I said.

"Is there not a government branch that dedicates itself to such matters?" he asked reasonably.

"Yeah," I said, adjusting a pillow under my knees, "but they don't think there's any spying going on."

"Is there?"

"I'm getting $48 a day plus expenses," I said in answer.

He nodded, understanding, and I sat up. My back was feeling better and through the window I could see that the rain had taken a break to load up for another attack.

"Back to work," I sighed. Gunther nodded, climbed down from the chair and went back to his room. I had three friends: Gunther, who said little; Shelly Minck, the dentist I shared an office with and who never made any sense; and Jeremy Butler, my office landlord, former wrestler and part-time poet. Jeremy was so big and ugly, he never had to say anything he didn't want to say. I had never tried to get the group together. I was afraid we'd be taken for a remake of *The Unholy Three*.

Putting on my second suit, a too-heavy blue gabardine, plus a robin's-egg-blue tie with just a touch of real egg still on it, I ventured out again into the late afternoon. The thunder rumbled a threat, and the little girls were back outside jumping rope and practicing to be witches under the protection of Mrs. Plaut's porch.

The toothless kid was turning the rope this time, and a new girl was jumping. One of her dark pigtails flopped on her shoulder; the other was held tightly in her mouth. Toothless chanted merrily:

Last night and the night before
Twenty-four robbers came to my door,
And this is what they said:
"Buster, Buster, hands on head;
Buster, Buster, go to bed;
Buster, Buster, if you don't,
I'm afraid they'll find you dead."

My faith in the future generation restored, I ambled to the Buick, patted the list of names and numbers in my pocket, and headed for Culver City and a freshly built, elongated two-story white antiseptic building with cheap but pleasant-smelling carpets. Anne Peters, née Anne Mitzenmacher, lived there. Well, she used it as an address. It didn't look lived in. If I put my clothes down in a place for twenty minutes, it looked lived in. If Anne spent five years in a single room, it would never look lived in. I found a parking place next to a dripping frond that bounced with joy at the moisture on its fat-ass leaves. I straightened my tie, pushed the bell and listened for the soft bong far away. It was after five and if she was coming home, she would be there. If not, I was on my way to the office, if a twenty-minute detour can be considered on the way.

The buzzer sounded, and I leaped for the inner door, I hurried up the stairs and to the hall. She was waiting and, as usual, not at all happy to see me. At least she didn't slam the door in my face. One time when she did that I had stumbled around the hall pretending to be drunk and singing "Annie, Annie was the miller's daughter, far she wandered from the singing water." She didn't like attention called to her, and she didn't like to be called Annie. She had opened the door that time, but the victory had been a hollow one. She had refused to talk to me when she let me in and actually called the police after giving me ten minutes.

I waited through five years of marriage for Anne to get fat like her mother. She didn't. Anne had remained full, dark and beautiful. Her hair was long and when she opened the door this time she wore a happy white dress with puffy shoulders and a not-too-happy look on her face.

"Business visit," I said, holding up both of my palms as I moved forward. She backed away to let me into her apartment. Her arms were folded, which was not a hopeful sign.

I stepped past her into the apartment. She hadn't changed a thing in the living room since I had last seen it. It was furnished with a modern brown chair and sofa, a light-brown carpet and tasteful brown wallpaper. On the wall was a painting of two factory workers shaking hands. Anne had always been a realist.

"Annie, don't you ever feel like throwing your bra on the floor and just leaving it there for a week or two?" I said in greeting.

"Never," she said closing the door behind me. "Business."

"You're looking great," I said, sitting on the uncomfortable-looking chair. "What happened to the executive you were going to marry?"

"I never said I was going to marry Ralph, you assumed that. Toby, I'm not going to let you goad me into battle. I've had a tough day at work and I want to be left alone."

On the sofa was a copy of *The Keys of the Kingdom* by A. J. Cronin with a golden bookmark about one-third of the way in.

"I saw Hughes today," I tried, my eyes watching her for that glint of interest. I caught it before she could cover up, and she knew it. She sighed and sat down.

"Toby, that doesn't buy your way into my life again." She sat stiffly, but her body quivered, and I smiled politely. She talked fast, "Ralph mentioned that Mr. Hughes had a problem and I mentioned your name."

"Annie. . ." I leaned forward.

"I mentioned your name," she said, putting Cronin on her lap for protection, "because they wanted someone who was discreet and reasonable. Fortunately, they didn't say anything about intelligence."

"You can't hurt me that way, Annie," I grinned.

"I know it," she said. "I threw you a job because God knows you can always use one. We have nothing to talk about."

"We have hundreds of battles, thousands of hamburgers, and years of apologies to talk about," I said.

She put the book down, walked to the door and opened it.

"Don't you want to hear what Hughes wants?" I said.

"I want to hear," she said softly, "but I don't want to pay the price for it. Your price is always too high, Toby. You can make a person live a century in fifteen minutes."

"And you used to love it," I tried.

She shook her head.

"I never loved it. I accepted it. We've been all through it, Toby. I'm almost 40 years old. I have no family, no kids. I've got a career and some hope. You don't cheer me up when you come around. You just remind me of everything I've missed."

"You sent me a perfumed letter," I said, getting up and moving toward her.

"I pay my gas bill with perfumed letters," she said. "I buy it by the box. Come on, Toby, I've had a bad day. My feet hurt and I have to look in the mirror soon."

"You're beautiful, Annie."

She shook her head and smiled sadly.

"I'm holding on, Toby," she said. "I heard someone in the office describe me as a handsome woman today. That depressed me almost as much as this visit is. Please take your needs someplace else. I'm not an emotional gas station that can keep pumping it out."

It had gone all wrong, and I was depressed and feeling sorry for her and myself.

"I tried," I sighed and went toward the door.

"Yes," she said softly, "but did you ever stop to think about what it was you tried and why?"

I stepped toward her, and she held her hand out looking like Kay Francis. It would have been a great lobby poster.

"I'll see you," I said.

"Take care of yourself," she said.

On the way back to the car, I decided to visit my nephews some time soon. Christmas was on the way. I'd get the boys the Foto-Electric Football game I saw advertised at Robinson's for $4.95. I'd get my sister-in-law Ruth a jacket from Bullock's. I'd get Phil a bottle of Serutan with a clipping of the ad that said "I'm 46 but I look and feel younger." I'd cheer everybody up. I'd be dear old Uncle Toby. Like hell I would. That wasn't the way to put Anne's words out of my mind.

Even Burns and Allen on the car radio didn't help. Three tacos and a large Pepsi didn't help. I was getting desperate enough to get to work. I pulled out the sheet from Hughes. The closest person on the list was Basil Rathbone. He lived at 10728 Bellagio Road in Bel Air, which wasn't too far. I spent a nickel and got Rathbone's wife on the phone. After I told her Howard Hughes had given me the number, she told me her husband was at NBC rehearsing a radio show. I thanked her, considered myself lucky that I wasn't too far from NBC and got back in the turtle and head down Sunset.

NBC looked clean, neat and sterile enough to have

been decorated by my former wife. Even the girl at the reception desk looked too clean to be real.

"Clarise," I said, leaning over confidentially to read her name tag, "my name is Peters. Mr. Rathbone is expecting me."

Clarise examined a skewered spindle of papers in front of her, searching for a note, a hint, a hope, an affirmation. I stood impatiently looking at my watch. My watch told me it was 2:10 in the afternoon or 2:10 in the morning. Neither was within seven hours of the truth. I wound the watch but it didn't help. Time stood still but Clarise didn't.

"For Mr. Rathbone?" she said.

I looked at the grey-haired guard behind her in exasperation.

"Look, young lady," I sighed. "I have about one hour between planes. Mr. Rathbone wanted to see me about production of the play. I did not want to see him. Our backers in New York don't think his name will mean that much to us, and we have an adaptation of *The Keys of the Kingdom* as a major possibility. Why don't you just tell Mr. Rathbone that I came by, you did your job and kept me from him, and he can contact me some time about the play. Just tell him it was Mr. Peters from the Schubert's in New York."

I turned to leave. I could have sat down and done some message sending. I could have waited outside for Rathbone to make an appearance. But I hadn't been able to resist the urge to con my way into NBC. Professional pride.

"I'll give Mr. Rathbone your message," she said.

I turned to give her a withering stare and a closer

examination. She was thin, vacantly pretty with frizzy auburn hair and in some other orbit. I tried another ploy.

"Where is the regular girl on this desk?"

Now how a man from Schubert's in New York would know she wasn't a regular would have been a reasonable question, but I had gauged Clarise's vacant look properly.

"She's on a dinner break. I'm just taking over for half an hour."

I pointed my finger at her and talked through my teeth. Maybe I could reduce her to tears and get back at Annie through womankind in the pathetic form of Clarise.

"What's your last name, Clarise?" I said.

"Clarise Peary. I usually work the telephones on. . ."

I wrote Clarise Peary's name in my expense book right under the nickel I had spent on the call to Rathbone's house. Clarise squirmed inside her dark blue NBC jacket. I had discovered back in my cop days that people didn't like having their names written down.

"Well," she hesitated, "if Mr. Rathbone is expecting you. . ."

"He is not expecting me," I said, leaning forward, not very proud of myself for intimidating a part-time clerk, "he is anxious to see me while I am not in the least anxious to see him. My time," I said, noticing again from my watch that time had stopped at two-ten, "is valuable."

"Paddy will take you to the studio," she sighed, looking anxiously at a couple who had come through the main door and were heading for her desk. She clearly feared having to handle two questions at the same time.

"Thank you," I said officiously. She smiled, showing

a crack in her face powder. The guard with the grey hair nodded and started down the hall toward a door. I followed him. He opened the door and I stepped through.

"You know," he said with a faint Scottish accent, "that talk wouldn't have fooled the regular girl for a second. Schubert's, hell." He chuckled.

"Then why aren't you tossing me out?" I said, hurrying to keep up with him as we went past glassed-in rooms of equipment and jacketless men with earphones.

"My name's Whannel," he said. "Worked at Warner's till last year. Got fired for drinking on a job—a job you got me sent on."

"I remember," I said. "Flynn. You and another security guy named Ellis were supposed to watch Errol Flynn. He got you drunk."

"And we got canned," he said, pointing to a thick wooden door. Above the door was a sign reading "On the Air." The sign was lighted.

"Then why didn't you turn me back at the desk out there?"

"Getting fired from Warner's was the best thing ever happened to Jack and me. NBC has better pay and hours, and I don't have to walk all over that damn lot. Be quiet when you go in there. They're not on the air, just rehearsing. Take it easy."

"You too," I said, and he left me. I walked into the studio as quietly as I could. It was a bigger room than I expected, with a stage and a small darkened space for about 30 chairs. I took a seat in one of the chairs. A handful of people were listening to the rehearsal.

On the stage was a slightly raised platform with a microphone and two men standing at it with scripts in their hands. To their left was an organ, but no one was there. To their right was a small flight of four steps leading to a contraption that looked like a glassless window. On the platform behind the steps was a wheel mounted on a table with a handle in the center of the wheel so it would be turned. Another contraption on wheels next to it held small wooden doors, one on each side, and next to the steps was a wooden box filled with sand. A man was standing in the box, with a script in his hand.

Behind the two men at the microphone was a glass partition with three men seated behind it all wearing earphones.

"Take it from the top of four, Nigel," came a voice. "One more time and then all the way through."

A portly man with a grey mustache wearing a dark suit and vest nodded. I recognized him from dozens of movies as Nigel Bruce. At his side stood Basil Rathbone in a tweed jacket and sweater. Rathbone looked out into the audience and directly at me, as if he knew me, and then turned back to the script.

Bruce let his face become perplexed so he could fall into character and said something like, "Rain had always depressed him when he wasn't working on a case," and the man in the box shuffled his feet, ran up the four stairs and opened one of the doors.

Rathbone said something like "Aha, we have a visitor," and the show went on with Rathbone as Holmes discovering a mad old killer named Amberly, who has gassed his wife and her doctor to death in a sealed room. Up to the last minute, I suspected Professor Moriarty, even though he had nothing to do with the episode.

After the announcer stepped forward and reminded the dozen people in the audience that "A little cold may be the start of a serious illness," I vowed to take his advice and buy some Bromo Quinine Cold Tablets. The show came to an end, and the director's voice came across tinny and cracked, saying, "That's good enough for day. Thanks Basil, Nigel."

Rathbone smiled and waved toward the glass partition, and Bruce nodded. A guy in the audience ran up on the platform to help the sound-effects man wheel away his props, and a woman with a script in her hand started to talk to Bruce. Looking less thin than he did in the movies, Rathbone walked directly toward me with his hand outstretched. I would have guessed he was a few years older than I was. His grip was firm and up close he gave the impression of being both agile and solid.

"You must be the man who so urgently has to see me," Rathbone said as precisely as he spoke on the radio, though a bit faster. "Let me guess what it's all about. You are a representative of Howard Hughes, conducting some kind of investigation about our dinner last week. Your investigation concerns something violent or potentially dangerous. It does not involve any danger to my person, but it does involve something to do with national security, or at least Mr. Hughes thinks it does."

Rathbone took out a silver cigarette case, offered me one, which I refused, lit his own and looked at me with some amusement.

"Pretty good," I said, as Nigel Bruce and the woman moved past us saying good night to Rathbone, "Holmes couldn't have done it better."

Rathbone laughed and ushered me out into the hall.

"Holmes," he said, "had a little trick which I have learned. He withheld obvious information and disclosed things in an order designed to surprise his audience. My wife called me and told me someone had called and mentioned Hughes and that she had told him I was rehearsing. The only contact I have had with Hughes in the last three years was at his home last week. He talked about the war and seemed particularly agitated. When I saw you sitting in the audience, clearly a man who has known violence in his life as evidenced by your visage, I began to put things together. You are not a policeman or you would have so announced yourself. You did not rush over here. Hence, my life was in no danger. So I took a few chances and sounded a bit like Holmes. I amuse myself at it occasionally. Would you care for a cup of coffee or tea?" I said yes, and he guided me into a lounge with leather chairs where a couple in their early 30's were whispering in the corner. The woman was hiding tears and the man pretending he had not seen us.

Rathbone and I went to a table, and he disappeared for a few minutes to return with two cups, one with tea, and one with coffee.

"You drink coffee normally," he said, "but today you are quite willing to drink tea."

"How did you know?" I said, drinking the tea while he took the coffee.

"Elementary My Dear. . . ."

"Peters, Toby Peters."

"Peters," said Rathbone. "You paid particular attention when Mr. Knox read our commercial for cold tablets, leading me to think that you had a cold or feared one. Then as we walked here it was quite evident that you held yourself a bit erect as if you had a tender back, possibly a cold in your lower back. If I may add, the condition of your clothes indicates that you are not particularly wealthy. Therefore, you need the money Hughes is paying you and probably have a fear of growing ill and not being able to collect it or do your job. Like most Americans, you equate tea with healing and believe it has some kind of medicinal effect. Therefore. . .''

''Thanks for the tea,'' I said. ''Let's talk about the Hughes party.''

''Gladly,'' he said, sipping his coffee. ''Hughes is an odd creature and rather commanded me to show up at his party, which almost decided me not to go, but he called personally and said it had something to do with the war effort. I've been working particularly hard to get Americans to support the British effort. I know what the Germans can do. I was in the last war you know, and I have a rather vicious scar on my leg where the barbed wire caught to prove it. I also have the memory of my brother John, who died in that war, and my mother, who never recovered from the shock of John's death and died soon after. Be patient with me Mr. Peters, I have a fondness for detail, but you'll see it all has a point in the end.''

I started to protest, and glanced at the couple arguing in the corner. Rathbone continued with his voice lowered.

''I watched Von Richtoffen and Goering destroy one of our planes in a field in France one afternoon. I saw. . . well, never mind. I've had premonitions from time to time. Had one just before John died, and I have had one for the past week. My feeling is a particularly ominious one. Do you believe in premonitions, Mr. Peters?''

I drank my tea, accepted a refill from Rathbone and shrugged.

''I believe in what I feel and what happens,'' I said. ''I believe in right now, not yesterday. Yesterday's memories are filled with regrets and tomorrow doesn't look too good. Right now I've got a hot cup of tea in my hand. I'm doing a job I know, and I like it just fine. Premonitions are fine with me, Mr. Rathbone.''

''Basil, please,'' he said with a smile.

''Basil. I have all I can do to handle facts and follow up ideas one at a time until they lead me somewhere or nowhere. What I do doesn't take a lot of brains, as my ex-wife reminded me tonight, and it doesn't take premonitions or deductions, just a lot of talk, some hard knocks and time.''

Rathbone scratched the back of his neck and went for another cigarette. He smoked Dominos.

''Well, Mr. Peters. . .''

''Toby,'' I said, evening up the first-name game.

''Toby. I seem to have caught you on a difficult day. Would you prefer to continue our discussion tomorrow? I have rather a light schedule this week, though next week I start shooting another film.''

I laughed, but it was a short laugh.

''Sorry,'' I said. ''I'll get professional again. Hughes thinks someone tried to steal plans for a couple of his planes at that dinner party. Did you see or hear anything that would support that belief? Any strange behavior by the guests? Any strange guests?''

''My turn to laugh, Toby,'' Rathbone laughed. ''They

were as unlikely a group to gather as Moriarty's band. Hughes had some idea of starting a coalition of patriots to support his plans for military tooling up. He has a rather boyish charm about him when he wants to, and who knows when I might be working in a movie for him? The Grustwalds were particularly nervous, though. They were tense and while appearing most effusive about Hughes' ideas, I would say they were the least interested. Their minds were elsewhere. I'm certain Hughes sensed this as well. The Army major was obviously drunk most of the night, despite his attempts to hide it. He functioned as a yes-man that evening for Hughes who, I would guess, found the man a mistake. Let's see. Most of the talking was done by Norma Forney, a rather caustic woman who writes for Twentieth, I believe. She was the most aggressive person at the gathering and also the least secure. She was witty, defensive and made me most uneasy—almost as uneasy as her escort, Mr. Siegel, whom she introduced as a businessman. I think I've seen him before but I can't put my finger on where. He seemed delighted to be there and worked hard at controlling a life-long lower-class New York accent. Our dress was as varied as our backgrounds. I wore tweeds quite similar to these, Hughes a suit too big for him and Siegel and Gurstwald tuxedoes. Hughes had neglected to tell us what to wear. I saw little of the servants other than a Japanese butler who seemed so conspicuously disinterested in all of us that I decided he was either feeble minded or very interested. Since something happened soon after dinner, presumably the problem which brings you here, Hughes never made his appeal to us. He was obviously distraught, had lost interest in his original idea, and sent us packing. That is about all I can say."

"It's a start," I said. "Anything else?"

"We, the guests that is, had pheasant and champagne. Hughes ate a salad and ice cream. He also sat further away from us than we were to each other, leading me to believe that Mr. Hughes has some aversion to people and tolerates them rather than likes them. I rather had the impression that he thought we were unclean and that he didn't want a great deal of contact with us, which leads me to conclude that he is a precise man. I'd be inclined to take note if a man like that told me something was wrong."

I got up, said thanks and Rathbone walked me down the hall toward the lobby.

"Toby," he said quietly as we shook hands in front of Clarise and Whannel, "I'm not sure I could be of any help to you, but I'd appreciate it if you'd let me come along with you on some of your investigation. Several reasons. If there is a security issue, I'm interested. I tried to enlist in the British army last year, but they turned me down, too old. Imagine that. I can outduel a twenty-year old. It would also give me some insight, as the resident Holmes, into how a real detective functions."

"Sure," I said, loud enough for Clarise to regain her confidence. "I'll give you a call tomorrow."

Rathbone left me and walked back down the hall. I nodded to Whannel and touched the tip of my hat to Clarise. I hadn't shaken the depression Anne and my back had hit me with. Instead of heading home, I caught the late show at the Hawaiian. *Citizen Kane* didn't make me feel any better about myself so I stopped for a hot dog at a Pig 'n Whistle and went home to bed.

CHAPTER FOUR

On Tuesday morning, I shaved and finished off half a box of Shredded Ralston while Tom Mix's picture on the box cheered me on. I tried to look like Orson Welles in the breakfast scene in *Citizen Kane,* but it was no go with Shredded Ralston. I gave up impressions and I listened to the radio while I got dressed. My back felt better.

I tried not to pay attention to the war news. The rest of the news was a toss-up. Beau Jack had beaten Mexican Sammy Rivers on a TKO in the third in Brooklyn. Someone had accused LA Chief Deputy District Attorney Grant Cooper of bugging the mayor in City Hall. George Murphy had the flu. We were going to get more rain.

I went to the hall phone with a pile of nickels, and started calling the people on Hughes' list. Major Barton didn't answer. Benjamin Siegel's butler, who could have used elocution lessons, said "the boss" was out for the day, but he'd leave a message. Norma Forney's office said she was in a conference, but I could call back. The Gurstwalds were home, and after three minutes, Anton

Gurstwald came on the line and agreed to talk to me "if Hughes really thinks it necessary." I said Hughes thought it was essential, and he grunted and told me to hurry over, since he had work to do in the afternoon. Mrs. Plaut gave me a broad smile as I passed her on the porch and went into the grey morning. It wasn't raining yet, but it soon would be. The Gurstwalds lived on the outskirts of a town called Mirador, not far from Laguna Beach off the Pacific Coast Highway. Since Hughes' house, at least the one he had been using for the party, was also in Mirador, I could talk to the Gurstwalds and the Hughes' servants, thus cutting through five-ninths of my list in one day, which would be enough work to award me the evening off so I could invite Carmen to the wrestling matches at the Eastside arena. There were six matches, with top bill going to Chief Little Wolf and Vincent Lopez. I'd splurge and buy the 75-cent seats and watch Carmen build up to a blood lust, which usually took her about two hours. The prospect cheered me on through Santa Monica, Torrance and Long Beach, where the rain hit fast and hard. By Newport Beach, the rain had stopped and a heavy, humid heat had collapsed on the world.

I turned off the highway at the Mirador exit and in two minutes found myself on the town's main street. The street was wide and almost empty. An automobile door of unknown vintage lay in the middle of the street with a grey cat on top of it. The cat was on its back with its paws up, waiting for the sun. A kid sat on one curb watching the cat and me and scratching dirt from his neck. Behind him were four or five stores that looked abandoned. On the other side of the street, two cars were packed in front of three stores, one of which, called "Hijo's" displayed a bulging live Mexican in a plaid shirt and cowboy hat. He looked at me and not the cat. Next to Hijo's was a small brick building with a sign in the window saying "Mirador Police." The windows were blocked by venetian blinds, but some cops were probably there, because a yellow Ford with a star painted on it was parked in front of the building.

Two other stores were boarded up, and another store had "Live Bate" hand-painted in green on its window. The green paint had dripped down the B forming a tail.

I pulled over to the kid with the dirty neck and got out of the car.

"Know where the Gurstwald place is?" I asked, helping him watch the cat.

The kid nodded yes. The next job was to get him to share the information. From the smell, I could tell we were close to the ocean. I could also hear the roll of waves in the distance.

"Think you might tell me?" I said, still looking at the cat. The Mexican in Hijo's window stirred and got up. I watched him for a few seconds until he looked directly at me, and then I turned my attention back to the cat on the car door. I pulled out a quarter and held it out where the kid could see it.

"Thirty cents," said the kid.

"I can find out for nothing from the cops," I said. The kid shrugged. He was skinny, dark and dirty, but he had class. He just kept looking at that cat.

"All right," I said. "Let's not quibble about a nickel."

"We ain't quibbling," said the kid. "We're negotiatin'."

I gave him the thirty cents, and he told me how to get to the Gurstwald place. For another dime, he told me how to get to Hughes' house after I gave him the street number. The big Mexican in the cowboy hat had stepped out of Hijo's, put a toothpick in his mouth and started across the street toward us, neatly circling the car door. He was either heading for the kid and me or the empty stores behind us.

I started for the car.

"Hey," said the Mexican, pointing at me with his toothpick. "You. What you doin'?"

"I'm getting in my car and heading for the Gurstwald place," I explained. "What are you doing?"

The Mexican came right at me out of the sun, and I could see the badge on his shirt for the first time.

"I think you better answer me," he said. "What are you bothering the kid for?"

"Shit," I sighed as quietly as I could, but he had good ears.

"Who you callin' shit?" he demanded.

"No one," I said. "I'm not looking for trouble. I'm just visiting some local residents."

"We don't get many visitors," he said, putting one hand on the fender of my Buick to keep the car from going away till he was ready.

"I can see why," I said opening my door. He kept his hand on the fender.

"Good," he said. "Just do your visiting and drive on through when you're done."

I turned the motor over and shook my head.

"That's too bad," I said. "I was thinking of picking up a few pounds of live bait."

The Mexican tipped his hat back and bit a small chunk off his toothpick. Then he examined what was left of the wood and spoke.

"Better to forget the bait than be it," he said softly.

"Didn't I see you in a Republic Western a few years ago?" I said seriously.

"I think I don't like you," he replied, spitting out the toothpick.

The kid had been watching us with such interest that he forgot about scratching the dirt from his neck.

"I don't argue with people who carry guns," I said. "Now if you'll just remove your hand, I promise to treasure the print and never clean it."

I swerved past the cat on the door and watched the Mexican deputy and the little kid grow small in the rear view mirror. I thought I saw a figure come out of the police office, but it might have been someone coming from the "bate" shop or "Hijo's". Whoever it was, I could do without further Mirador hospitality.

The Gurstwald home was about two miles back on a paved road on a cliff over the ocean. It looked like it had a few dozen rooms. It certainly had a large brick wall around it with a heavy metal gate. It seemed an unnecessary precaution, since no one could find the place and no one seemed to live anywhere near it. The Gurstwalds valued their privacy.

I parked at the side of the gate and walked towards it. A well-built young man with short blond hair, wearing denims and a blue cotton shirt with long sleeves rolled up to show his muscles, stood on the other side.

"My name's Peters," I said. "Toby Peters."

The young man nodded, opened the gate and motioned for me to move ahead of him up the gravel path. I moved.

"Nice place," I said.

"Yes," he said, adding nothing. I shut up and walked to the door. He opened it and I stepped in. He stayed behind me.

There was a stairway in front of us and a man descended, wearing a scarf and lounging jacket. He had grey hair cut almost to the scalp, and he must have been somewhere in his sixties. He was either wearing a fat jacket or he could have done with the loss of thirty or forty pounds.

"Mr. Peters," the man said with a distinct German accent. "In what way can I serve our Mr. Hughes?"

He shook my hand amiably and indicated a room to his right. I went in, followed by Gurstwald and the blond with the muscles. The room was bright and looked out on a flower garden. I had expected something dark and somber with pictures of the Black Forest on the wall. Instead, I found a thick white carpet and yellow wicker furniture.

I sat in a chair with a paisley cushion, and Gurstwald sat across from me in its twin with his hands gently clasping his knees. The muscleman stood behind me. I did not feel comfortable in Mirador. I felt as if I had driven into a foreign country when I left the Pacific Coast Highway, and I wanted to leave that country with everything I had entered with. I decided to be careful and discreet. Sometimes being indiscreet can get a lot done, but the wear and tear on the human body is enormous.

"I'm an investigator working for Mr. Hughes," I said, trying to include the silent muscleman in the conversation but finding it impossible with him at my back. I gave up and concentrated on Gurstwald. "He was hoping you could help us with a problem. When you were at Mr. Hughes' home last week for dinner, did you notice any unusual behavior by any of the guests or servants?"

Gurstwald looked puzzled.

"Unusual?"

"I'll spell it out, Mr. Gurstwald," I said leaning forward to show how I was taking him into my confidence. "Mr. Hughes has reason to believe someone in the house that night may have stolen some valuable plans and . . ."

Gurstwald's face turned a bright crimson and he rose slightly from his chair, glancing at the blond behind me.

"You don't mean to accuse me of . . ."

"No," I said quickly, having no intention of accusing a man with a bodyguard in the middle of nowhere. "We don't suspect you of anything. We simply want your help in trying to find the guilty party."

Gurstwald calmed slightly and sat down again. He straightened his scarf, took a deep breath and asked if I wanted something to drink. I said I'd like a Pepsi. Gurstwald nodded and the blond disappeared.

"Mr. Peters," Gurstwald said, "you've been frank with me. I'll be frank with you. What has Mr. Hughes told you of me?"

"Nothing," I said, which was true.

Gurstwald touched his lower lip with the fingers of his right hand, nodded to himself and spoke, choosing his words carefully.

"I am in a difficult position, Mr. Peters. My family has been in the munitions business in Germany for almost 100 years. For political reasons, which must be quite obvious to any intelligent man, I broke with my family and moved much of my operation to Mexico about five years ago. The financial loss was tremendous for me, but I could not exist under the Third Reich. There are still many in your government who have difficulty accepting me and my wife, though I have offered to work with your military people in developing certain operations.''

''For a price,'' I added, a bit more confident without Adonis in the room.

''Yes,'' Gurstwald said, loosening his scarf. ''For a price. I am a businessman. So is Mr. Hughes. He was interested that we might form some kind of cooperative venture when the war begins. I must admit that, though I do not approve of what is happening in my country, I have certain misgivings about actually contributing arms to the United States in case of war. My position, you understand, is quite delicate.''

''Certainly,'' I said, accepting a large glass of cola from Adonis. The ice cubes crackled and I took a gulp. It was Royal Crown, but I didn't complain. ''You live out here because you don't want to attract attention.''

''Precisely,'' he sighed, pleased that I understood. ''Various countries and corporations try to get me to cooperate with them, but my position is quite delicate, as I said, so I try to keep to myself, protected to a degree.''

''Including a payoff to the Mirador cops to discourage strangers,'' I tried, gurgling RC.

''You had an encounter with our police,'' he sighed. ''I'm so sorry, but you understand.''

''Clearly,'' I said. ''Now, what did you see, if anything, at Hughes' last week?''

Gurstwald clasped his hands, bit gently into his lower lip and said, "Nothing. Precisely nothing except that Mr. Hughes seemed particularly disturbed after dinner. Everyone else was delightful."

Maybe Gurstwald had seen nothing, but I wondered. I wondered just how delightful Major Barton had been. I also wondered what was bothering Anton Gurstwald. It might be just what he said, but it might be something else.

"Good enough," I said, finishing the RC.

"Another," said Gurstwald with a phony smile.

"No thanks, but I'd like a quick word with Mrs. Gurstwald."

Gurstwald got up quickly, and the red returned to his face.

"But she can tell you nothing," he chuckled nervously. "She noticed nothing. And she is resting."

"O.K.," I said, getting up, determined to talk to Mrs. Gurstwald, "I'll stop by and see her after I talk to the servants at the Hughes house."

"That won't be possible," Gurstwald said emphatically. "She will be busy all day."

"Right," I sighed in resignation. "It's a long ride, but I'll come back tomorrow."

"I do not think you should disturb Mrs. Gurstwald at any time," he said with heavy Germanic emphasis.

"Right," I winked. "I'll just tell Mr. Hughes you wouldn't let me talk to her." I started toward the door with my back to Gurstwald, who had a hurried conversation in German with Adonis.

"Mr. Peters," Gurstwald said, "perhaps Mrs. Gurstwald can give you a moment or two now, but I tell you she knows nothing.'' The enormous shrug of his shoulders made me want to hear that nothing.

Gurstwald hurried out of the room, leaving me with Adonis, who gave me a quick, artificial smile and then simply watched me to be sure I didn't steal a wicker chair.

About five minutes later, Gurstwald returned with Mrs. Gurstwald who looked like an Olympic ski champ. She was almost as tall as I was and had short, curly blond hair. She was well tanned, perspiring, and wore a white tennis suit, which was strange attire for someone who was resting. I guessed she was around thirty. Her teeth were large and white and her handshake gentle but firm. She was definitely pretty in a healthy milk-ad way, and something was on her mind.

``My dear,'' Gurstwald said, leading his wife into the wicker-and-flowers room, ``this is Mr. Peters, and he is investigating some possible wrongdoing at Mr. Hughes' house when we were there last week.''

``I see,'' she said, with less of an accent than her husband, but an accent nonetheless. It was a toss-up as to which of the pair was the worst actor.

``I have told Mr. Peters that we saw nothing suspicious,'' Gurstwald said, rubbing his hands together. ``Everyone was very compatible.''

``Very compatible,'' she echoed, looking at me.

``Well,'' said Gurstwald, ``you have it. I'm sorry we could give no more help.''

Politeness had gotten me nowhere, and I was convinced there was somewhere to get with the Gurstwalds. My initial idea had been just to contact possible suspects and get some kind of feeling about them. The feeling I got from the Gurstwalds was that nerves were crying to be prodded.

''Right,'' I said, walking toward the hallway. ''You've given me a lot to think about. Like why I make you so nervous you have to concoct a little show of 'I-saw-nothing' for my benefit. You're hiding something, Gurstwald, I can smell it with this bashed nose—the bashing taught it how. I don't like secrets, and I'm going to find yours if it has anything to do with Howard Hughes.'' I turned to watch the effect of my speech on the Gurstwalds. She had almost lost her tan. He was flushing through pink, red and white and he reminded me of the Albanian flag. Or was it Luxembourg? Gurstwald nodded to Adonis, who moved forward quickly to take my arm. I let him. Mrs. Gurstwald hurried out of the room, and Gurstwald slowly regained his normal pinkish color.

''You have insulted my hospitality, Mr. Peters.''

''You going to slap me with a white glove and tell me to meet you at the Hollywood Bowl with my seconds?'' I said.

''You are not to bother me or my wife again,'' he said, quivering. ''You are to stay away from us and not meddle in our affairs. We will have our privacy at any cost.''

Adonis' grip tightened.

''May I take that as a threat?'' I asked politely.

Adonis pushed me toward the door. He was young, strong, and confident and he expected no trouble from me. He was wrong. I turned toward Gurstwald as if to speak and unloaded a left to Adonis' midsection. The air poofed out of him, and he collapsed, grasping his stomach and trying for air.

Gurstwald looked angry, then scared.

"I'll be seeing you again Anton."

I hurried into the hall and out the door. In a fair fight, I might not be a match for Adonis. I didn't want to stick around for a fair fight with a 25-year-old refugee from a Wagnerian fantasy.

I slammed the door and started down the path, but a loud whisper stopped me. I debated a run for the car, but curiousity turned me. I didn't become a pillar of salt. The whisper was Trudi Gurstwald at the corner of the house.

"Mr. Peters," she said. "I have something I must tell you. Where can I reach you?"

"My office is in Los Angeles. The number's in the phone book under private investigators. I'll be there tonight."

She disappeared and with her my hope of getting Carmen excited at the wrestling matches that night. If Trudi Gurstwald had something to say, it might be worth the loss. I felt pretty good as I jogged the twenty yards or so to my car.

I caught a few minutes of some soap opera advertising Hormel Chili, which reminded me that I was hungry. I tried to forget it as I continued down the road in the general direction of the Hughes house, according to the directions from the kid in Mirador. It was no more than a mile from the Gurstwald place, which seemed a hell of a coincidence. Hughes' place was smaller than Gurstwald's, with a nice lawn and a great view of the Ocean. It was a big red brick lump of a house trying to look like something English. I drove up to the door, got out and rang. It took about thirty seconds for the door to open.

The opener was Japanese, in his late twenties and wearing a white jacket.

"Yes?" he said. I caught no accent in the answer.

"Name is Peters, I'm working, like you, for Mr. Hughes and I've got some questions."

"Right," he said, stepping back so I could enter. "My name's Toshiro. Mr. Dean called and said we might be hearing from you. Mind if we talk in the kitchen? I was making myself some lunch."

I said sure and followed him into the house, down the hall and into the kitchen. He had some onions and tomatoes on a wooden counter and a large can of tuna, half open.

"Like a sandwich?" he said.

"I'd like two," I said.

He nodded and worked while we talked.

"Work for Hughes long?" I asked, sitting on a stool near the table.

"About three weeks," he answered, opening the can and forking the white chunks of tuna into a bowl. "You like mayonnaise?"

"Yeah, as much as you can tolerate. You've only worked for him three weeks? What about the other servants?"

"Same," he said. "Hughes just rented this place to set up a dinner for a guy down the road named Gurstwald who has even less love of company than Hughes. Normally, I'm a grad student at Cal Tech, but I take off every once in a while to make a few dollars. This seemed like a good deal."

He held up a bottle of Rainier Beer from the refrigerator, and I nodded yes. So he pulled out one for himself too.

"Where are the others, the cook and the butler?"

"Schell, the butler, is out," said Toshiro, opening the Rainier. "Nuss, the cook, is in, but he got bored and drank himself to sleep. We're all waiting to be canned and meanwhile collecting our pay for sitting around."

I picked wheat bread and Toshiro joined me. We ate quietly for a few minutes and sipped our ice cold beer.

"I think Hughes really lives in the Beverly Hills Hotel," he said, emptying his beer bottle. "I get a lot of reading done here."

"What about the night of the dinner party?"

Toshiro got us both seconds on the beer.

"Hughes stayed the day before. Brought a guy named Noah and a couple of well-dressed bruisers. Stayed in his room going over stuff he brought in an old briefcase. Nuss made him an avocado and bacon sandwich for dinner and Schell brought him some crackers and milk around three in the morning."

I gurgled some more beer and leaned forward to put some salt on half a tomato I was nibbling.

"Night of the big blast," Toshiro continued, "Everything went as scheduled. We actually had a typed schedule right down to when we circulated with drinks."

"What'd you make of the guests?" I said. Toshiro shrugged.

"Money," he said. "They've all got it except maybe that major. He's got a problem in a bottle. Which reminds me, another beer?"

I said yes and we downed a third.

"Well," he resumed, leaning against the sink,

''everything was routine till Hughes went up to his room about an hour after dinner to get something. When he came back, he called the servants into the kitchen, changed the schedule and shuffled the guests out as fast as he could.''

''How'd they take it?'' I burped. ''Sorry.''

''Fine, except the Gurstwalds, but they seemed kind of odd the whole night anyway. Something was eating them. You know. They were just irritable.''

''They say they had a great time,'' I said.

Toshiro shrugged.

''Well maybe, I've never seen them having a bad time.''

''You going back to Cal Tech when this job ends?''

Toshiro raised his eyebrows and carted dishes over to the sink.

''A guy named Toshiro might have a rough time around the states for a while if Japan gets a war going. I might just be better off getting a job around here and riding it out. Maybe I'll even join the army. But that would be tough on my parents. We've got lots of relatives in Japan.''

''Where are your parents?'' I said.

''You grilling?''

''Yeah, I can't help it.''

''Parents live in San Diego.''

I got up and let Toshiro show me Nuss the cook sleeping in his room. His clothes were on and he smelled of wine. He also hadn't shaved in a few days. Toshiro closed the door behind us as we left.

''Seems like a decent guy,'' Toshiro said leading me

to the front of the house. "The butler, however, is not one of my favorite people."

"What's his problem?"

"Don't know," said Toshiro, opening the front door for me. "Strong silent type. Looks at everyone like they were ants and he was a big shoe. Not the kind of guy I'd want for a butler, but no one asked me."

"Thanks for the lunch and beer," I said, stepping out into the humidity.

"Howard Hughes' compliments. Drop by anytime."

The door closed behind me, and for about four seconds I felt swell. At the end of that four seconds I noticed the car parked next to mine. It was the yellow Mirador police Ford. Leaning against it was the Mexican cowboy. Next to him was a wiry little guy in a sweaty lightweight suit who was wiping the sweatband of his straw hat with a moist handkerchief. He looked like he was around forty, and he squinted as if the sun were particularly bright, which it wasn't. Then he spotted me, put his hat on and gave me a fake grin.

"Mr. Peters?" he said, advancing on me while the Mexican watched passively.

"Right," I said.

"I'm Mark Nelson, Sheriff of Mirador. You've already met Alex, my deputy, which means you are acquainted with the entire constabulary of Mirador." He chuckled and I chuckled back. Nelson moved to my side and put a hand on my shoulder and his head near mine. He smelled like onions. We walked a few feet from the car while he whispered confidentially.

"Was a time Mirador looked as if it would be a big

resort area," he said. "Look around at these trees. Listen to the ocean. What has Laguna got that we haven't?"

"I give up," I said.

"Developers," he whispered confidentially through his teeth. "People willing to make a commitment to the community. We had a couple of them before the Depression back in '28, but it fell through. We've even got a big hotel almost finished on the beach. Looks just like it did back in '30."

I looked around at the trees and listened to the ocean. Then I looked at Alex, who looked at me.

"There's a point to all this, isn't there?" I said, "and I'm going to get it soon?"

Nelson took his hat off and did some more work on drying the stained hatband of his straw hat.

"Right," he said, pointing a finger at me and smiling. "I'll get there soon. And I'll try not to bore you. What we have in Mirador instead of fancy resorts and shops with junk, is a handful of people barely making it and another handful of very rich people who like Mirador because it is peaceful and secluded."

"Like Anton Gurstwald?" I guessed.

"Just like Mr. Gurstwald," he confirmed.

"And people like Mr. Gurstwald are willing to pay a few extra bucks each month or so to insure that privacy?"

"You are a smart man," Nelson said, shaking his head in appreciation. "We'd prefer that people who are not wanted by those who value privacy respect that wish. Now you've intruded on one of our leading citizens and assaulted a resident."

"I'm also working for another resident," I pointed out. "Howard Hughes."

"Right enough," said Nelson, "but a man has to make decisions, a sheriff has to make decisions and sometimes they aren't easy ones. Now Mr. Hughes is really just renting his privacy and he doesn't pay those few extra dollars to insure it."

"He just pays his rent and his taxes," I said, "and those are supposed to give you some rights without kick-back."

Nelson shook his head sadly.

"I believe you are becoming slightly abusive," he said. "I was hoping we could handle this without abuse. I'm going to have to insist that you leave Mirador and never return."

I looked deeply into his very moist grey eyes, and he looked back steadily. I had to give him that. He could hold a gaze with the best.

"And suppose I don't give a shit what you insist?" I whispered.

"Ah, well then, let's pretend I told you a joke. Here's the punch line."

And I got the punch line from Alex, who has stepped silently behind me. He hit me in the right kidney and sent dry ice up my spine. My bladder, filled with three beers, almost let go, but I held on and slipped to my knees.

"I got it," I gasped.

"Good," sighed Nelson. "I hoped you would. Please help the man up, Alex."

Alex helped me up and handed me my hat. I staggered, considered hitting Alex with something, ideally with Sheriff Nelson, and changed my mind.

"Well, it has been nice meeting you, Mr. Peters. Maybe we'll run into each other in the city some time."

"I'd like that," I said.

Alex opened the door of my Buick and helped me inside. Nelson squinted up at the sun and moved to the open window.

"By the way," he whispered again, "Alex and I noticed that your car had a little accident, front bumper's been ripped off by a vandal. Alex stuck it in your back seat."

"Thanks," I said, making a mental note to charge it to Hughes and give him a full account of what happened. "Anything else that might affect my transportation?"

"No, no," he grinned, stepping back so I could drive away, "we wouldn't let anything happen that might prolong your stay in Mirador. Now you know the way out of town, but just in case, we'll follow behind as an escort."

"I appreciate that," I said, trying not to wince from the pain above my kidney. I needed a toilet or a clump of trees fast, but I wasn't going to find a hospitable place in Mirador.

The drive back to and through Mirador was uneventful. The kid wasn't on the curb and the cat was gone, but the car door was still there. There were two more cars parked in front of Hijo's, but I didn't pay any attention. I just watched Alex and Nelson in my rear view mirror. They stopped when the street turned to road, and Nelson stuck his hand out the window to wave goodbye.

I didn't wave back.

CHAPTER FIVE

I found a Sinclair station on the highway, told the guy to fill it up and made a Groucho dash to the men's room. The dash resulted in pain and relief, along with a feeling of satisfaction. I had some decent leads paid for with a firm belt in the kidney. Maybe that evened the score with Fate and the Gods. They let me have a little information and I paid for it in pain. It was a deal the Gods and I had had for almost thirty years, and we both understood it. I would have felt uneasy if things came without a price. I think I inherited that from my father. It was probably the only thing I inherited from the poor guy besides a watch that wouldn't tell time.

I paid the gas station attendant who looked like Andy Devine, asked him the time and drove back toward Los Angeles humming "Chatanooga Choo–Choo." My back was being reasonable.

I drove to Arnie's garage on Eleventh Street and told no-neck Arnie, whose face was so thick with grease that he looked like something from the road show of *The Jazz Singer,* that he should get my bumper back on as soon

3/2/06

as possible. Arnie shifted his stub of a cigar and grunted. He never asked how bullet holes, blood and ripped bumpers appeared. He just fixed and charged.

I legged it over to my office, trying to ignore the memory of Alex's kidney attack and stand up straight as I walked. I made it to Ninth, passing Montoya the Dropper, a neighborhood character who would walk about thirty feet, only to repeat the thing over again. Montoya refused to acknowledge that he kept falling and became indignant if anyone confronted him with it. This affliction caused Montoya some professional difficulty since he made his meager living as a pickpocket. He was certainly the world's most conspicuous pickpocket. I also passed Old Sol. Old Sol walked around with a whistle in his mouth and a book in front of his eyes. He blew the whistle whenever he came to a streetcorner and traffic stopped, green light or not. Since Old Sol was about seventy and he was still healthy, he was apparently doing something right.

They were two of the more savory characters of the neighborhood I met as I turned down Hoover to the Faraday Building, the four-story refuge for second-rate dentists, alcoholic doctors and baby photographers where I had my office.

As usual, the dark hall smelled of Lysol. Jeremy Butler, the former wrestler and present poet and landlord, spent a good chunk of each day fighting a losing battle to keep the building clean by carting squatting bums out the back door and slopping on pails of Lysol. He also changed the light bulbs regularly, but they were constantly being stolen or substituted for lower wattage by the tenants.

The Farraday Building had an elevator, but only the uninitiated took it. Few people could afford the time the trip took. I echoed up the steps and down the hall to my office. The window on the outer door had been cracked and replaced where my landlord had thrown a troublemaker through it, a troublemaker who tried to rob Sheldon Minck.

The neat black letters on the glass read:

SHELDON MINCK, D.D.S., S.D.
Dentist
TOBY PETERS
Private Investigator

The door was new, but the reception room had been embalmed years ago. There was enough space for two wooden chairs, one once-leather-covered chair, a small table with an overflowing ash tray and a heap of ancient copies of *Colliers*. There was a whitish-grey square on one greyish white wall, where a dental supply company chart showing gum disease had recently fallen after a decade of doing its duty and warning the populace.

I hurried along through the alcove into Shelly's dental office, a single chair surrounded by old dental journals, coffee cups that should have been cleaned and piles of tools in various states of rust. Shelly's radio was playing Smiling Jack Smith. Shelly himself, in a once-white smock and thick glasses slipping off his moist nose, was working on someone in the chair. Shelly shifted his cigar and turned his fat, bald head in my direction.

"Toby, you got a call. I don't remember who."

"Thanks Shelly," I said and moved across the office

toward my own office, which had once been a small false-teeth lab.

''Hughes'' said a voice from the dental chair. It was Jeremy Butler. ''The call was from someone named Hughes.''

''Right,'' agreed Shelly, pushing his glasses back and humming with Jack Smith as he looked for some instrument among last week's newspapers.

''Jeremy,'' I said. ''Since when do you let Shelly work on your teeth?''

Butler shrugged his enormous shoulders and leaned back, resigned.

''I was reading in the paper today,'' Shelly observed pulling out a mean looking tool, ''and I saw this big ad for that dentist, Doctor Painless Parker with offices all over the coast, and I said that's what I'd do. I'd advertise. Where the hell are those pliers?''

''What else d'you read in the papers?'' I said, being friendly.

''Dick Tracy's caught in a snowstorm.''

''Terrific,'' I said.

''You working?'' Butler asked softly. Usually, Butler spoke barely above a whisper, but people listened. People usually do when you weigh 300 pounds and most of it is muscle.

''Yeah,'' I said, happy to have a sounding board. I pulled up a stool, removed the newspapers from it except for one little corner that stuck to something wet and sat down facing the dental chair. Shelly found his pliers and I gave a quick summary of the case, talking over Jack Smith warbling ''Just One More Chance.''

I pulled out the list from Hughes. Butler examined it slowly and Shelly took a quick glance.

"It's the Jap," said Shelly, turning with his pliers to Butler. "If not the Jap then the Nazi dame Gurstwald."

"Thanks for clearing it all up for me, Shelly. You are invaluable."

He waved his pliers, indicating that it was nothing much and was about to attack Butler's mouth when the big man rose.

"I've changed my mind," he said, removing the dirty white cloth from his neck.

"We had a deal," Shelly protested.

"You can still take five dollars from your rent," said Butler. "It's getting late and my sister's boy is coming to spend the night with me." Shelly sighed and put his pliers down.

I was curious about Jeremy's nephew. I wondered if he resembled a bathtub like his uncle.

"How is the new place working out?" he said, meaning Mrs. Plaut's rooming house. I had been renting a small motel-like bungalow from Butler before that.

"Fine," I answered. Shelly climbed into his own dental chair with a newspaper.

"Take care of yourself, Toby," Butler said and out he went.

"I'm closing down early," Shelly said looking at his cigar. "Mildred and I are going to see that all-Negro musical at the Mayan, *VooDooed*. You want to come?"

Jack Smith paused so I could answer.

"No, I'm waiting for a call. Mind if I use your radio when you leave?"

He said he didn't mind, and I went into my office to

check on the mail, which didn't exist, look at the framed copy of my dusty private investigator's license, examine the photograph of my father, my tall heavy brother and our beagle dog Kaiser Wilhelm. I hated and loved that photograph and the ten-year-old kid in it who had been Tobias Leo Pevsner. My brother Phil's arm was around my shoulder in the photograph, my father looked proud. My nose was already smashed flat by Phil, and Kaiser Wilhelm looked sad as he always did.

Shelly left just before six and I went down for three burgers from the stand at the corner and brought them back to my desk with a Pepsi. I put in a call to Hughes through Dean at the Romaine office and sat eating as I waited for Hughes to call me back and Trudi Gurstwald to get in touch. I listened to Shelly's Silvertone radio while I munched and turned to KFI for a jolly night of Burns and Allen, Fibber McGee and Molly, Bob Hope and Red Skelton. By the time Bob Hope came around, Hughes had still not called. In the middle of Red Skelton, I heard someone come into the outer office. I wasn't expecting trouble, but I didn't feel like taking chances. I had left the light on in Shelly's office and my small light off. I snapped off the radio and tiptoed to the door to open it a crack and peeked out.

I saw Trudi Gurstwald, her little yellow curls bobbing, in a fresh dress looking clean and fluffy. It contrasted with her pink and anxious face. She looked around the room nervously and made a turn to leave. I stepped out.

"Mrs. Gurstwald," I said, and she turned, startled.

"Mr. Peters," she said, her accent strong. "I thought I had missed you. I have only half an hour or so. Anton thinks I am shopping and I must meet him at 8:30. I have a cab waiting downstairs.''

She paced the room and I took a seat in the dental chair. The surroundings didn't seem to surprise or bother her. She had something else on her mind.

''I don't know what Anton would do if he knew I had come here,'' she said, looking at me earnestly.

''I don't either,'' I said. ''Why don't we put it from our minds while you tell me what you wanted to tell me about that night at Hughes' house.''

She bit both of her lips and turned to me with moist eyes.

''I'm really afraid,'' she said taking a step toward me.

''Well, lady,'' I came back, ''you may very well have reason to be afraid. You have my sympathy, but I can't give you anything more till you tell me what you know.''

She took another step toward me, almost crying.

''You can't know what it is like living there with Anton and those people,'' she said softly, her eyes searching mine. ''He has such fear of the Nazis, the Americans, so many people. He can think of nothing else. And he has no strength left for me. He had such strength, Mr. Peters.''

I nodded knowingly, deciding to let her talk it out in the hope that she'd get to the point herself. After all, she was the one who had the cab waiting.

''When you came this morning,'' she said, ''it was the first life in that house in months. You said things no one says to Anton and you did to Rudy what I've wanted to do for years.''

The tears were overflowing, and she was standing over me in the chair. I half expected her to pick up one of

Shelly's contaminated instruments and go to work on me. Instead she leaned over and put her open mouth on mine. Her mouth was large and engulfed me to the point where I had trouble breathing.

She let me up for air and I caught some, but she wasn't breathing hard.

"I haven't even touched a man in years," she whispered.

I felt sorry for her, but she didn't give me much time to feel anything. She took my face in her hands and placed her mouth back on mine. I was in an awkward position for getting up, but I had the impression that even if we were on equal footing, Trudi Gurstwald was a match for me. Besides, I didn't dislike what she was doing. I was just puzzled by it. I had learned to distrust the few women who had found me irresistible. There always seemed to be a price to pay for it. On the other hand, I never really had the will power to turn down the attention. It came too infrequently. So I didn't try to stop Trudi Gurstwald and did my best to enjoy her kisses, while being curious about where they would lead to and wondering whether she was crazy and how long she'd let the cab wait.

Her hands moved down my chest to my legs and then between them, and I stopped being curious. She may have been desperate and distraught, but she was doing the work. I gave her some help, and she moaned loud enough to wake any of the bums who might have been sleeping in the halls.

We wrestled cooperatively around the dental chair getting my pants down and her dress up. At one point her breasts battered my head against the head rest and almost knocked me out. I had a fantasy of Trudi Gurstwald going up against Chief Little Wolf at the Eastside Arena and taking him in two falls.

Making love in a dental chair—if that was what we did—is definitely not recommended for someone with a bad back. It has its rewards, but it also has it consequences. I was exhausted when Trudi Gurstwald gave me a final smile through her tears, kissed my sore mouth and stood up.

"Thank you," she said sincerely.

"My pleasure," I said, trying to stand up and finding myself pushed back in the dental chair by the pain in my kidney. I pulled my pants on in a sitting position and tucked in my shirt. Trudi looked at me soulfully and I thought she was going to have another attack of emotion. I wasn't sure I could survive it.

"Trudi," I said, pushing myself from the chair and taking her hand before she could take mine or some other part of me. "What did you see at Hughes' house that night?"

She looked at me in surprise and straightened her hair and then remembered one of the points of her visit.

"It was that Army major," she said.

"Barton."

"Yes, Barton. I went upstairs that night to the—how do you say it politely?"

"Toilet."

"Yes, toilet. Someone was using the downstairs toilet and I saw this Major Barton coming out of a room. The door opened enough so I could see it was an office with papers and drawings. Major Barton was nervous and looked around both ways to see if anyone saw him coming from the room. I was in the . . ."

"Toilet."

"Yes, I must remember that word. It is awkward to say Powder Room when one doesn't mean Powder Room."

"Major Barton," I prodded.

"He looked both ways, closed the door and went down the steps. He had sweat on his head, and he wiped it with his sleeve, though the night was cool."

She squeezed my hand and looked soulful again.

"Anton was afraid I should tell you and he would get involved," she said. "I had told him. He said it would be the questionable word of two Germans against that of an American officer. But I had to tell you. If someone finds out we knew and said nothing, and it turned out to be important, we would be in even bigger trouble."

"Right," I said. Her eyes were growing moist again and I added, "You've been here about half an hour. You've got Anton and a cab waiting."

"Again soon?" she asked.

This time I kissed her first.

"Again soon," I said and guided her to the alcove, where she tripped against the once-leather-covered chair.

When she stepped into the hall, I locked the door behind her to keep her from a sudden change of mind. I wasn't worried about her being attacked by any of the neighborhood bums. She could take care of herself.

I figured it was about nine and was about to turn on the radio to find out, when the phone rang.

"Peters," I said.

"I say this once," the voice said in sharp Germanic

English. It was a man's voice and it was not a patient voice. "You cease your current investigation. You cease or soon there will be no Toby Peters."

"Shelly," I said. "Is this your idea of a joke? Your Hitler is as bad as your Clark Gable."

"This is no joke," hissed the voice. "And you would be wise to heed my warning."

"I don't know who's doing your dialogue, pal," I said, "but it could use a rewrite."

He hung up before I could. I knew it could have been a gag. But I also knew there was a chance that it wasn't, so I calmly got my things together, put on my jacket, turned out the lights and decided to go home and sleep on it.

I got as far as the alcove door when I saw the shadow in the pebble glass behind the reversed lettering of Shelly's and my name. It looked like the shadow's owner had something in his hand. I stepped back and whoever it was tried the door I had locked behind Trudi Gurstwald.

"We know you are in there, Peters," came a voice suspiciously like the one on the phone. "We called from across the street. Now open the door and we will have a nice talk without disturbing people."

His use of the editorial "we" failed to convince me that someone was with him. On the other hand, he seemed to have a gun and mine was in my car's glove compartment.

"Look," I said, backing away in the hope of making it to the phone, but the "look" was as far as I got. The figure in the hall put two shots through the window, shattering Shelly's name and mine. The bullets hit somewhere in the general vicinity of the whitish square where the gum disease chart once rested. I remember thinking we'd have to put the chart back to cover the bullet holes, and then I realized the bullets had come within a hair of hitting my face. The guy with the gun had been waiting for my voice so he could fire toward it. I backed against the wall, reaching for one of the alcove chairs. There was an open square where the window had been and it showed the hall. I saw no one there. But I heard no footsteps. Stupid anger took hold, and I went for the door like a Neanderthal, with chair in hand. Chair against gun. Idiot against achiever.

I opened the door, pushing glass out of the way, and stepped into the hall. Whatever he hit me with, and I think it was the gun, was right on target, low on the skull. I went down, knowing he had suckered me into the hall while he pressed himself against the wall.

I didn't go out right away. My hand must have automatically dropped the chair and went to the back of my head to keep in the blood or stop another blow. I rolled over on my back and dimly saw a guy above me with a gun. I had never seen him before. He reminded me of a fuzzy version of Ward Bond, and then I was out.

Koko the Clown took my hand and led me into the inkwell where we found ourselves in Cincinnati. He drove me up the side of the hill across the river and out to the suburb in the hills where I lived. Then Koko disappeared. I ran to my two-level house to greet my family, but they weren't there. I ran outside and they weren't there. I ran past rows of shacks and no one was there. I was alone in Cincinnati and scared. I was scared because no one else was alive in Cincinnati and because I've never been in Cincinnati in my life and I wondered even while I dreamt what the hell I was doing there. I think I also wondered if I was dead. Someone groaned, and Koko reappeared to take my hand. He led me to my car, with the bumper still missing because Arnie hadn't gotten to it, and drove me back down the hill and out of the inkwell.

Early morning sunlight burnt my eyes and I forced them open. I was still alive, or as close to alive as I usually am. The chair I had taken into the hall was a few feet away. The glass from the broken window of my office was all over the place. The back of my head screamed, and I remembered a warning from Young Doc Parry about not taking any more jolts in the head. I managed to sit up, wondering what time it was and why I was still alive.

The door to our offices was open and so was the door to the alcove. From my sitting position, I could see Shelly's dental chair, the same chair where Trudi Gurstwald and I had tussled minutes or hours ago. Someone was in the chair, and that made me wonder. If Shelly had a patient in there, he must have seen me in the hall. He was insensitive, but not enough to leave me out there. He'd at least wake me to complain about the broken window.

My eyes focused slowly and I recognized the man in the chair, though there was something strange about him and the way he stared at me. The something was that he was dead and covered with blood. I started to crawl toward him, remembered the glass on the floor and pulled myself up, using the open door. Then I touched the back of my head and discovered that there was no blood, just a massive lump that would end my hat wearing for a few weeks.

I made it to the guy in the chair, the guy who I had thought looked like Ward Bond. He didn't look like Ward Bond anymore. He looked like a frightened corpse. His eyes were open and his tongue was sticking out. Blood was on his sleeve and he held a gun tightly in his left hand. His right hand rested on top of Shelly's porcelain work space next to the chair. The junk on it had been swept to the floor, and the marble-colored porcelain was covered with drying blood.

I started to make my way toward the phone when I noticed that his right hand was pointing at the blood on the table. I shook my head clear, let some water trickle onto my hands from Shelly's sink and splashed it on my face. Then I looked where the dead man's finger was pointing. In blood he had written something that looked like "unkind."

It seemed a conservative description of what had happened to him.

CHAPTER SIX

I called my brother and told him I had another corpse for him. He didn't rant. He didn't rave. He just said he would be right over. I looked at the phone, wondering if I had reached the right Lieutenant Philip Pevsner, the one who turned purple, lived in rage and took crime and me as a personal affront.

The pain in my head and the knowledge of the character in the dental chair behind me kept me from dwelling on Phil. I flipped on the radio and found it was eight in the morning. Shelly had part of a one-pound can of Ben-Hur coffee he had picked up at Ralph's for twenty-eight cents. I made some, trying to avoid the guy in the chair. Then, to keep my mind from the pain and funny white spots I kept seeing, I went through the corpse's pockets, careful not to disturb the position of the body. He had a wallet. The wallet said he was Louis Frye, that he lived in Covina and that he was thirty-eight years old. He had thirty bucks and some change. He also had a telephone number written on a torn off corner of newspaper stuck among the dollar bills. It was a familiar number. I checked it against the list Hughes had given me. The number belonged to Major Barton. I left the number and dollar bills in Frye's wallet and put it back in his pocket.

I was just starting my coffee when Phil and Steve Seidman came through the door, followed by a big bald uniformed young cop named Rashkow. Sergeant Seidman, a thin cadaverous-looking character with a notebook, didn't say much at any time. This time he said nothing, just went to the body and began examining it. Rashkow took a quick look, gave me a grin but wiped it off when Phil caught it.

"Suppose you step out in the hall and keep people out of here," Phil said evenly. Rashkow nodded, and Phil gave the messed up room a disgusted look and pointed toward my office. I went. In a few minutes, Shelly's office would be full of people with cameras, bad professional jokes about death, and medical bags.

Phil closed the door to my office behind us and looked at me, pursing his lips. He was a little taller than I was, a little broader and a little older. His cop's gut was developing gradually, and his close-cut steely hair grew greyer every time I saw him. Normally, he had the look of a lunatic who required superhuman effort to keep in his rage. Today he wasn't the old Phil.

"How are Ruth and the boys?" I tried. For some reason, that had always driven him over the top into a rage. I normally saved it for telephone conversations. It was safer. I supposed the rage was caused by the fact that I never came to visit him, my sister-in-law and the kids in North Hollywood.

Phil didn't get angry. He put his hands behind his back

after loosening his tie and looked at the picture of him, me, our father and Kaiser Wilhelm.

"How long's it been since you saw Ruth, Toby?"

Considering the corpse in the chair outside, it seemed an odd direction for the conversation.

"A few months," I tried.

"Make it almost a year," he said, his back still to me. "It's two boys and a girl now. Ruth had a baby while you were in Chicago. Her name's Lucy."

"That's great," I said, wondering why a forty one-year-old woman and a forty seven-year-old cop with less salary than a cab driver would have three kids. Then I thought of Anne and decided to say nothing. Phil turned around and took in a greath breath. If he let it out in one burst he could have huffed and puffed down the Farraday Building.

"Who's the guy in the chair?"

"Name is Frye," I said, sipping my coffee. "Want some coffee?" He shook his head no so I went on. "He came up here last night and took a couple of shots at me. That's what happened to the windows."

"I hadn't noticed," Phil said sarcastically. "The place looks the same as when I was here last."

I finished the coffee, winced a little from the pain in my head and went behind my desk to sit.

"He took a couple of shots at me, and I went out in the hall after him with a chair, but he put me away with a crack on the head, and I didn't get up till I called you a little while ago."

"How'd he get in the chair?" Phil asked reasonably.

"I don't know."

"Who killed him?" Phil tried.

"Don't know."

"Why did he try to kill you?"

"I don't know."

"You are a fountain of information," Phil sighed, his rage starting to return. "How did you know his name?"

"I went through his pockets just before you got here. Nothing there." I didn't mention that the phone number in the corpse's wallet was Major Barton's.

"This is a silly question," he said, "but has anyone got a reason to want to kill you? I mean, I know a lot of people would like to stamp on your face a little, the line forms behind me, but anybody particular? You working a case?"

"I'm working a case," I acknowledged.

"Think you might tell me a little bit about it?" Phil said, moving over to sit on the wooden chair across from my desk. The potential rage was in check and I was having trouble dealing with the new Phil.

"Can't tell you much without an O.K. from my client," I said.

He nodded knowingly. Outside we could hear the bustle of cops and a "Hi Doc" greeting for the guy from the Coroner's Office. Phil just looked at me while I pretended to drink some more Ben-Hur coffee, though the cup was empty.

The phone rang. I let it ring. Phil pointed to it and then to his ear. I picked up the phone. It was Howard Hughes.

"You have something?" he said, coming directly to the point.

"I think so," I said, looking at Phil, who waited patiently. "But I can't talk now. A man named Frye came looking for me with a gun and got himself killed. The police are here now, and they'd like some information about what I'm working on."

The pause on the other end of the line made me think I had lost him, but his voice came back steadily.

"I do not want to be involved in any publicity," he said. "My name is not to be mentioned. If you mention me, I'll have to deny it. If you keep me out of it, you get a bonus."

"How much would that be?" I said, looking at Phil.

"Two thousand and fifty," he said.

"Dollars?" I said.

"I don't deal in any other currency."

"I'll do what you want, but no dollars. I'd do it for any client."

"I prefer to pay," he said.

"There are one or two things you can't pay for," I said, looking at Phil, who was starting to show signs of impatience such as adjusting his tie constantly.

"I'd like a report tonight at midnight sharp," Hughes said, and then he gave me an address. I said right. Then I hung up and looked at Phil.

"The client?" Phil said evenly.

"Right."

"And he doesn't want to cooperate with us."

"Right again," I said, shaking my head sadly.

"I see," said Phil.

Seidman knocked at the door and walked in without waiting to be welcomed.

"Lieutenant," he said. "It's a weird one. The guy out there is covered with blood, but it's not his. Doc says there's not a wound on his body, not a cut. He was strangled. And it looks like he wrote something in blood on the table next to him before he went.''

''Unkind,'' I said.

''Something like that,'' Seidman agreed.

''Terrific,'' Phil sighed, looking at me. ''And you can't explain any of it?''

''No,'' I said sadly.

Seidman tilted his hat back to reveal more pale dome and added, ''Guy's gun's been fired four times.''

''Must have hit whoever strangled him,'' I said.

''Brilliant,'' Phil nodded.

As Seidman made a discreet exit, Shelly burst in, his face red and his mouth open.

''How was the show?'' I said.

''Show?'' he answered, pushing his glasses back in confusion.

''*VooDooed,*'' I reminded him.

''Fine,'' he said. ''What happened out there, Toby?''

''Cleaning lady came early,'' I said.

''Cops, blood, a dead guy in the chair, the doors are broken again. I've got patients coming in half an hour. How's it going to look with a dead guy in the chair?''

''Terrible,'' I said. ''The police will clean him out as soon as they can.''

Shelly was not appeased and he mumbled, ''I've got a pregnant woman coming in at nine-thirty. How's this going to look? Who's going to pay?''

I pulled out my wallet, counted fifty from the money Hughes' man had given me, and handed it to Shelly. He took it and walked out, still mumbling.

''Maybe this'll do some good after all,'' I said to Phil. ''We might get the place cleaned up.''

Phil was looking sad. He got up, walked to the photograph of the family, touched my framed license and turned to me.

"I don't like mysteries, Toby," he said. "Why do you call me every time you kick up a corpse? The city is full of cops."

"You're my brother. I like to give you the business."

For a man who spent most his time behind a desk, Phil could move pretty fast. He proved it by crossing the small room in two steps, lifting me from behind the desk with his right hand and punching me firmly in the stomach with his left in less time than it takes to cross your eyes.

"I've had it, goddamit," he shouted, standing over me, "I've goddam had it with you."

I liked him better this way, but I had the feeling I had turned on something I couldn't stop. Seduced, shot at, clubbed, corpsed and beaten by one's brother in a few hours was enough for any man. So I just stood there against the wall, waiting for his next move.

"It's simple," he said, breathing hard. "You tell me about your client and everything else you know, or I stamp on you. You know I mean it." His finger was inches from my face, and I knew he meant it.

Seidman came in, saw me on the floor and spoke softly to Phil, who kept his eyes on me.

"Problem, Lieutenant?"

"No, Sam Spade here is going to cooperate, aren't you Sam?"

"No client's name," I said, covering my head with my hands and expecting a kick. When Phil lost control, he lost control; a kick was as good as a punch. I wondered how his kids and wife survived, though Ruth had once assured me my brother was a model father and husband and never hit his kids. Maybe he saved it all for the job.

"Lieutenant," Seidman said.

"All right. All right." Phil stood up and turned his back to me. "Book him. Suspicion of murder."

I pulled myself straight and wondered how long my body could take all this attention.

"Phil," I said with exaggerated calm. "You know I didn't strangle that guy. He shot whoever strangled him and I'm in one piece, it's a battered piece, but it isn't bleeding. And how can strangling be murder when the victim has a gun in his hand?"

"Sergeant," said Phil, "get him out of my sight and put him in the lockup for a few hours."

Seidman motioned for me to come, and I considered prodding Phil a little more. I had him back in form and I didn't want to lose him now, but something in Seidman's look changed my mind and I followed him.

In the outer office, a police photographer was snapping pictures of broken glass on the floor. The body had been removed, and Shelly was trying to put his tools together.

"That corpse had good teeth," Shelly said. "Real gold fillings. You don't see many of them in this neighborhood."

"I've just been arrested," I said. "For murder."

"You killed that guy?" asked Shelly, without looking up from his search for something on the floor.

"No, I didn't. I'll get back as soon as I can."

"Right," said Shelly, holding his glasses on with the finger of his right hand. Seidman led me out of the office.

"What do you get out of driving him up the wall?" Seidman asked as we walked down the stairs, absorbing Lysol and the looks of a few curious tenants and bums.

"I don't know," I said. "I'm just used to him that way. What does he get out of putting lumps on me?"

"Forget I asked," said Seidman, leading me out of the Farraday Building to a parked black and white police car. "I'll lock you up for a few hours. Then do us all a big favor and try to stay out of his way."

"I'll try," I said, "but he's irresistible."

They threw me in a cell with another dangerous criminal, a little guy in his sixties who was stewed silly at ten in the morning. I sat on the almost clean bunk, holding my head and counting backwards from 100 to keep from noticing the pain in my head.

"You can call me Calvin," the drunk said, sitting next to me. "Calvin means 'the bald' in some language. I looked it up when I was a kid, but I fooled them. I've got more hair than my father ever had. Take a look."

He shook me and I opened my eyes. I had been at 85. Calvin was smiling and tugging at his ample white hair to prove he had it.

"That's great, Calvin," I said, "but I've got one hell of a headache and . . ."

"They picked me up on Wilshire this morning," Calvin continued, ignoring me. "You know why I was drunk?"

"You consumed too much alcohol," I tried.

"I mean the deeper cause," he said. "It's the news. I got up to go to work and turned on the radio and this guy started telling me about someone trying to kill Mussolini, and about Roosevelt asking Japan to explain why they were concentrating troops in Indochina. And Roosevelt says peace depends on an answer. And more kids were being drafted into the army.''

I didn't see how an attempt to kill Mussolini necessarily came under the heading of bad news, but I didn't want to carry on a conversation with a drunk. I had some numbers to get through and some thinking to do. I had a pile of clues to a murder, but I couldn't figure them out, and besides I wasn't being paid to find a murderer. I had suspicious characters all over the place and too damn much information. I wasn't used to all this information. It probably would have given me a headache even without the lump.

''Was there any good news?'' I said.

''Yeah, Mel Ott is going to manage the Giants. Ever see him play? One foot up in the air when he bashes the ball.'' Calvin got up to demonstrate Mel Ott's unique batting style. He hit a triple which further cheered him and he sat again to keep me company. ''What you in for?'' he said groggily.

''Murder,'' I said, closing my eyes. ''I gutted three drunks on the Strip last night with my bare hands.'' I could feel Calvin rise slowly and move quietly to the far side of the small cell. I slept. This time no dreams, no Cincinnati, no Koko.

I got up because someone was shaking me, a cop. Calvin was snoring away in a second bunk.

''You're out,'' said the cop wearily. ''Lieutenant Pevsner wants to see you in his office.''

I got up and told him I'd find my way there. He told me I was getting an escort. Ten minutes later I was going up the steps of Phil's station in the Wilshire District, past the desk sergeant, up the stairs and through the big sour squad room. I had been accompanied by Officer Rashkow, who said nothing because I said nothing. He left me at my brother's door and I went in.

Phil was behind his desk, and Basil Rathbone was seated across from him. Rathbone rose.

"Mr. Peters," he said. "So sorry to hear what happened. I hope you're all right." He took my hand and held my shoulder.

"Mr. Rathbone has persuaded Captain Rein to let you go," said Phil, playing with an Eversharp automatic pencil, which he turned over and over and over. "Mr. Rathbone has also refused to tell us what he knows about this and why he is interested in getting you out. Mr. Rathbone knows we are investigating a murder."

"I also have no information, Lieutenant," he said sincerely. "I met Mr. Peters a few days ago when he visited a taping of my radio show. I promised to look him up and discovered when I called his office that he had been arrested. Then I simply made a few calls and . . ."

Phil kept spinning the pencil and nodding his head to show he understood but he didn't believe.

"Have it your way," Phil said. "Toby draws bodies like flies to orange pop. I'd suggest you stay away from him."

"I shall certainly consider your advice," Rathbone said as if he fully intended to consider the advice. "Now, if we may. . ."

Seidman stuck his head in the door before we could get permission or move.

"He's on," Seidman said.

"All right, I'll take it," Phil sighed, staring at the

phone. "You two can go. It's a friend of mine, a crank who's been calling every day for the last two weeks to threaten me. It makes my day." Phil picked up the phone and spoke into it staring at me. "Hello. You are? You are? I am? That's nice to know. Just keep talking. I know you won't be on long enough for us to trace, but do you mind if we try, just to keep in practice? Thanks."

Rathbone, who was dressed in a neatly pressed dark suit and matching tie, made a motion, and Phil put his hand over the receiver.

"Yeah," said Phil.

"Give me a try with him," said Rathbone, "maybe I can keep him going long enough for you to trace it."

"That's ten, maybe fifteen minutes, depending on where he's calling from, but he won't stay on long enough. O.K. Give it a try. What the hell." He handed the phone to Rathbone, who said:

"This is Basil Rathbone. Yes, the actor. I'm sorry if you think this is a poor imitation. It's actually me. I happened to be in the Lieutenant's office when you called, and I've never spoken to a lunatic before. My, my, my you needn't get insulting. I see. And how will you accomplish this? Grisly. But you don't even know the Lieutenant. How will you be sure you're not getting the wrong man? Oh, you do. Yes, Yes. That's a fair enough description. Must you? So soon? Well, if you must. Goodbye."

Rathbone hung up.

"Couldn't keep him on," said Phil.

"No," said Rathbone," but I did discover a few things about him that might help you to pick him up. He is a Canadian who has worked for a doctor or in a hospital or is a doctor; and he knew you, I would guess, about ten years ago. I'd suggest you check anyone you put to prison about ten years ago who recently got out and fits that description."

Phil started to rise from his chair.

"Levine, Edward Levine," said Phil. "Sent him up for assaulting a doctor in County Hospital where he was working in '32." Seidman came back into the office to indicate that they had not traced the call.

"Forget it," said Phil. "Check on Ed Levine. May have gotten out of Folsom recently. Check his parole officer, find him and pull him in. I think he's our man." Seidman nodded and left.

"The voice could be his," Phil said. "It's been ten years, but . . ."

"He have some special fondness for you, Philip?" I said. Phil looked up at me, and I went on. "Some good kidney chops help him confess? Ah, but you were a wild youth."

"Get out," he said. Rathbone and I got out. On the way through the station Rathbone absorbed the sight of drunks, looneys, cops and assorted hangers-on lounging around.

"Fascinating place," he said, as we stepped into the sunlight.

"Fascinating," I agreed. "How did you know all that stuff about the guy on the phone, Sherlock?"

"If we are to cement this friendship, Toby," he said with a smile, "please call me Basil. As much as I enjoy the profit of being Sherlock Holmes and am interested in the process, I fear I am, after thirty years as a Shakespearean actor, becoming identified with a character who may overwhelm my career. I'm getting a bit of a taste of how Dr. Conan Doyle must have felt when he tried to kill Sherlock off. I am, however, not at that point. As to the business on the phone back there, I owe it more to being an actor who spends a great deal of time studying voices than I do to a study of Holmes. I knew he was a Canadian because of the way he pronounced "ou" in words like "about," "out." Canadians pronounce these two letters as "oo" as in "too." Of course a small group of Americans in Minnesota do the same, but the odds were numerically with the Canadian. As to the medical knowledge, the gentleman on the phone described what he would do to Lieutenant Pevsner with an anatomical knowledge that would have been the envy of Jack the Ripper. Finally, the man's description of the lieutenant was easily ten years out of date. He described a man thirty pounds lighter and with hair just beginning to grey. He had not seen his intended victim for about ten years. Then I put it all together."

"You could have been way off," I said, letting him lead me to a blue Chrysler at the curb.

"My dear fellow, I could have been entirely wrong," he admitted. "Holmes, unlike us poor mortals, always had the fortunate protection of Dr. Conan Doyle, who would affirm almost every bizarre deduction the consulting detective made."

We got in the car and I gave Rathbone Major Barton's address, after briefing him on what had happened and getting his assurance that he wanted to come along.

"I called you this morning for the express purpose of accompanying you on some of the investigation," he said. "Tell me, do American police actually beat suspects, or were you simply prodding the Lieutenant out of some long-standing antagonism?"

"The antagonism goes back more than forty years," I said. "He's my brother."

"That explains a great deal," said Rathbone.

"The answer to your question is, yes, some, maybe most cops do use a little muscle to push a suspect into a confession or get some information. Being a cop is a tough job. I used to be one in Glendale."

"I see," he said. "The English aren't all that less barbaric. I'll make an anti-Holmesian confession to you. About fifteen years ago in England, I had an excellent manservant named Poole, who was an armed robber by night to supplement his income. He kept it up for some time, and I never suspected the fellow, even when they arrested him and he confessed. When he got out after serving his time, Poole told me that he had received nine lashes of the 'cat' for having carried firearms during the robberies. The cat, in case you do not know it, is a wooden handpiece to which are attached nine leather thongs soaked in oil. A prison doctor must be present because a single stroke of the lash can lay a man's back open to the bone. The lashes, according to Poole, could be given at any time, in any combination. They could pull a man out of his cell after a year at three in the morning, give him two strokes and send him back bleeding for minutes or months to await the rest. They've done away with the cat now, but I've met many who are sorry about its passing. So, perhaps the English are not so much more civilized than the Americans when it comes to treating criminals."

Major Barton's home was in Westwood, a small house set back on an untrimmed lawn. I didn't know if he was there, but I had gotten nowhere trying to reach him by phone, and Trudi Gurstwald plus his phone number in Frye's wallet had made him my A Number-One Suspect. It was worth a chance.

Barton was home. He answered the door himself and he was in uniform, or at least partly in uniform. His jacket, tie and shoes were not on and I had the impression we had interrupted him while he was dressing. He was about fifty, a little taller than I and working hard to keep his stomach in by will power instead of exercise. His nose had the red touch of a drinker, and his breath confirmed Hughes' information.

"Mr. Rathbone," he said in surprise. "To what do I owe this visit?"

"Good afternoon, Major," Rathbone said amiably, "this is Mr. Peters. He is working for Howard Hughes, and he'd like some help with something you may be able to assist him with. May we come in?"

Rathbone stepped forward the way he did as Holmes in *The Hound of the Baskervilles* movie, and I followed behind.

"I was just on my way out," Barton said, trying to get ahead of us to cover the mess and bottles in his living room.

"We won't take a moment," smiled Rathbone. "I'm sure you want to cooperate with Mr. Hughes' emissary."

"Of course," said Barton. "Just give me a minute to finish dressing, gentlemen. Make yourself at home. Have a drink."

We went into Barton's living room, and Rathbone immediately opened a window to let out the stale smell, then sat down comfortably. The room was small, darkly carpeted with a sofa and some chairs. The chairs looked expensive, far from new, and not recently dusted. They were striped black and brown and looked lived in. On the wall was a picture of Napoleon on a horse. The horse was up on his hind feet and Napoleon was looking at me with his sword raised before he joined the battle in the background.

Barton came back in a few minutes, smelling of Sen–Sen and after-shave lotion. But the alcohol still came through.

"Mrs. Barton is out of town for a few days," he said, having a seat. "Please excuse the condition of the house."

"This is confidential, Major," I said, pulling a seat as close to him as I could. "You're assigned to. . ."

"Special duty working with various aircraft manufacturers on proposals for new weaponry," he supplied. "Hughes Aircraft is one of those manufacturers."

"Good," I said. "Mr. Hughes has reason to believe that something may have been copied at his house the night of the dinner party, something valuable relating to the very weapons you're talking about. Did you happen to see anything suspicious?"

Barton thought for a few seconds and then came up empty.

"Sorry," he said. "Nothing happened out of the ordinary as far as I was concerned, though Hughes did behave a bit strangely after dinner and put a rather abrupt end to what I thought was going to be an evening of discussion. I think Mr. Rathbone will confirm that."

"I confirm your observation about Hughes," said Rathbone, staring at the man and taking out his silver cigarette case.

"Major Barton," I went on, "what would you say if I told you someone in the house that night has told us that they saw you coming out of Mr. Hughes' study shortly after dinner and that you looked nervous? What would you say?"

"I'd say they were a goddamn liar," Barton said indignantly, rising. "I'd say let them say that to my face."

"Well," I said, "maybe we can arrange that. It's gotten pretty important. You see, a guy named Frye was murdered this morning, and I think it's related to what happened at Hughes' house. You wouldn't know anything about that, would you, Major?"

Barton flushed and stood up, staring at the impassive Rathbone and at me.

"What made me think you might know, Major," I pressed on, "was the fact that Frye had your phone number in his pocket. Why was that?"

"I don't know," Barton gasped.

"The police have his wallet with your number in it. They'll be coming to see you soon themselves."

"I'll ask you to leave my house now, Mr. Peters," he said. "My record and my reputation are enough. . . ."

"To make a sailor blush," said Rathbone. "Tell me, Major, why are you still a major at your age? Shouldn't a West Point man have made Colonel by the age of fifty?"

"How do you know all that?" Barton started.

"Your West Point diploma is on the wall and the year of your graduation, indicating your approximate age,"

Rathbone explained. "Could your drinking have something to do with it? You do a very bad job of hiding it, you know. And where, pray tell, is your wife? From the look of this place, no one has taken care of it for some time except a gardener. No Major Barton, I rather fancy your job is not as important as you've indicated and that you've been given this assignment to keep you from embarrassing superiors or some influential friend who is protecting you. A military classmate, perhaps?"

Barton licked his lips, almost defeated, and Rathbone lit a cigarette, turning his eyes from Barton for the first time. Barton reached for a bottle and poured himself a drink. He didn't offer us one.

"I can't tell you anything," he said. "I'm going to report what I know to my superiors as soon as you leave, and they can do with it what they will. You'll get no more from me."

"I think we've gotten quite a bit," said Rathbone. "Perhaps you'll be more inclined to talk to us after you've seen your superiors."

"Perhaps," said Barton, "but I doubt it." He downed his drink and went silent.

Rathbone indicated that we should leave, and we did, but not before we saw Barton pour himself another drink. On the front steps, Rathbone said:

"Sorry about that, Peters, but I couldn't resist playing Holmes. I quite enjoyed it."

"That's all right," I said. "Except I started to feel like Watson, and that didn't do anything for my self-image."

"Well," he said. "Comfort yourself. Nigel plays Watson as much more of a loveable bumbler than Conan

Doyle intended. After all, Watson was very much Conan Doyle—doctor, admirer of ratiocination, solidly built. Our version is a bit more comic. Now I suggest we have something to eat and return in an hour to question Major Barton again, when he has made himself more vulnerable with drink and fear."

"You don't buy his tale about going to his superiors," I said, getting in the car.

"No," said Rathbone, getting in the driver's seat and pulling into light traffic. "I can't believe a West Point man, even one who tends to drink, would go to a meeting with his superiors with his shoes unpolished. He certainly wouldn't after having a few drinks."

We found a small steak place for lunch. Since it was after one in the afternoon, it wasn't crowded, and no one but the waiter stared at Rathbone. We ate, with him urging me to talk about what it was like being a private detective. It was nothing like being Sherlock Holmes.

"Well," I said, "for a month back in '39 I was a night bouncer at a hot dog stand in Watts. Four bucks a night and almost all you could eat.

"Later that same year I filled in for the hotel dick at a place in Fresno. One month again, room and board, mostly old women cheating at bridge. But one night we had a woman come running out of a shower screaming rape and I followed a trail of wet footprints down the hall and into a room. I found a guy in a closet. He scared the hell out of me, jaybird naked and covered with blood. Never did find out where the blood came from. The woman hadn't bled. Never found out how he got in the room or hotel either. He wasn't registered, and the room belonged to a priest who was in town for a convention and said he never knew the guy and had left his door locked.''

''What did the man in the closet say?''

''Nothing,'' I said. ''He turned out to be the father of a famous radio comedian. Fresno cops wouldn't tell me who, and they let him go. He hadn't raped the old gal in the shower, just turned up in there naked and bloody and scared hell out of her. And that guy's still wandering the streets of Fresno or L.A.''

''An entirely different genre,'' Rathbone observed, sipping a wine of uncertain vintage while I downed my second beer and made a mental note to get to the Y as soon as possible before my brother and I had matching beer bellies. On the way out of the steak place, the waiter asked Rathbone for an autograph and got it on a menu.

''For my wife,'' said the waiter, a thin guy with his hair combed straight back.

''It always is,'' said Rathbone when the waiter left.

He allowed me to take the check after I assured him it was on Howard Hughes.

We went back to Major Barton's little house with a good meal under our belts and almost an hour and a half behind us. It was late in the afternoon, and the sun was promising a hot Christmas.

I knocked but Barton didn't answer. I knocked again, deciding Rathbone had probably been wrong and Barton had gone with a couple of drinks and unpolished shoes to his superior officer to lay down his secret of the Hughes night, if he had such a secret other than his own spying.

Rathbone tried the door and it wasn't locked.

''Major,'' I called. No answer. We stepped in and found the major just where we had left him, in full uniform, glass in hand but with the addition of a pair of messy red stains on his shirt. Someone had shot him at close range. I'd seen a lot of corpses in my day and that day included the morning and the guy in Shelly's chair; but though I knew Rathbone had been in the war, I wasn't sure what he had seen. I turned, and he was looking around the room.

"You needn't worry about me, Toby," he said. "I had proximity to more corpses during the war than a man would care to have in a lifetime. Once I had to step on a decomposed corpse while running from the Germans. I've seen corpses, especially corpses in uniform—though never that uniform. . . . Curious."

"What?" I said.

"The neighbors," he said.

"What neighbors?" I said.

"Precisely," said Rathbone. "We left the window open when we departed and it's still open. There are people on the street. A bullet makes quite a bit of noise. Why isn't anyone here? Why aren't the police here?"

I looked at Barton but didn't touch him. There was nothing around that seemed to help.

"Might have used a silencer," I said.

"To kill quietly," Rathbone said, looking down at Barton. "A particularly chilling concept."

"He's been dead for more than a few minutes," I said. "Blood is starting to dry. So no one's called the police, and I don't think I'll stick around to do it. They don't like it when you discover two corpses in one day. How about we just leave here quietly and I make an anonymous call?"

"If you think it best," he said, and we left. Rathbone

had to get home and prepare for a dinner, so he drove me to Al's garage, and I promised to call and keep him informed.

The bumper was back on and I was short of suspects. My favorite had just been shot. Maybe he had passed on the Hughes plans to an accomplice who was afraid he would talk and killed him. Maybe he had seen someone else in Hughes' room and that person had killed him. And maybe one of these maybes had seen me and Rathbone coming out of Barton's. Or just maybe someone who had nothing to do with the case had killed him, but that would have been one hell of a coincidence. I believed in coincidences, but I didn't count on them. I always counted on my fingers and hoped I never had to go over ten on any problem, but this one required an adding machine.

I pulled in at a grocery store, picked up three boxes of Kellogg's Corn Flakes, 11-ounce size for 17 cents, three bars of Lifebuoy for 19 cents, and one pound can of Campbell's Pork and Beans for 7 cents. I also picked up a Weber's bread and a can of Bab-o. That and a bottle of milk was my grocery shopping for the week. Then I called the cops with my best Italian accent and told them where they could find a corpse named Barton. Finally I called Norma Forney at Warner Brothers. She didn't want to see me and laughed when I said she might be a suspect. After she made a few smart cracks, I said she reminded me of a Warner Brothers version of Dorothy Parker. She liked that.

I drove to the studio where I had put in four years as a guard. I had time for both *Superman* and *Don Winslow* on the radio because of the traffic, and I pulled up to the

Warner gate to the music of Bing Crosby singing ''Shepherd's Serenade.''

The guy on the gate was someone I didn't know. I just told him my name and the fact that Norma Forney was expecting me. He told me she was in an office near Studio 5, and I didn't wait for directions. I knew the way. The last time I had been there was to catch a murderer. I had left with the help of Errol Flynn and an ambulance. My memories of Warner Brothers were not the best, and I was anxious to be in and out of there. I found the building, parked in a space reserved for Hal Wallis, and hurried up to the office. There was no secretary. A woman was sitting behind a desk with a typewriter on it. Her hands were behind her head and a pencil was in her mouth.

''Norma Forney?'' I said. She looked up.

''Peters?'' she said through the pencil.

She was about thirty with a good-looking smart face and blue eyes. Her dress was dark, black, and made out of something shiny like satin. Her dark hair was cut short and she wore a small hat with a single long pheasant feather.

''You've got some inspiration?'' she asked. ''I could use it. I'm supposed to be adding gags to this script, *The Male Animal,* but I'm not feeling funny. I haven't felt funny since my gall bladder operation. Tried to make gall bladder jokes. There aren't any. What can I do for you—quickly?''

Since I wanted to be away from Warner's as much as she wanted me away, I talked fast, telling her about my investigation of the Hughes' theft, or possible theft, and left out the two murders.

"Can't help you," she said. "I wasn't even a potential contributor to the festivities, though I probably talked too much. I usually do. I got the reputation that I was a witty kid when I wrote my first and only play. I've been trying to live up to it ever since. That is one hell of a burden to carry, Peters."

"There are worse," I said. "Then why were you there?"

"I went with Ben Siegel. It was him that Hughes wanted to meet."

"Why?" I asked.

"If you're working for Hughes, why don't you ask him, or is he on his way around the world on a kite?" she said.

"Mr. Hughes doesn't talk very much," I said, and she nodded in agreement.

"O.K.," she said. "Hughes said that when the war broke out, he wanted Ben to organize some friends in Europe to act as a kind of information network. We were going to talk about it that night, but Hughes broke up the party."

"What kinds of friends does Siegel have in Europe?"

She looked at me as if I were from the hills of Dakota.

"Criminals," she said, "drug dealers, killers. Bugsy Siegel knows a lot of people."

"I didn't know it was that Siegel," I said.

She gave me a broad fake grin.

"You are one hell of a detective, Peters. Remind me to call you if I ever lose my mind. Now if you'll let me get back to my nonwork. . ."

I left, promising that I might be back. She said she was looking forward to it, but her eyes said she wasn't.

You can't charm them all. I left without seeing a single movie star or anyone I knew, which was fine with me.

My next stop was Bugsy Siegel's. I had a pair of addresses and some phone numbers. I called the first and got no answer. Then I called the second and got someone with raw fish in his mouth. I said I wanted to talk to Siegel. I don't know what he said, but he went away, and a few minutes later another voice came on.

"What do you want with Mr. Siegel, and how'd you get this number?"

"I'm working for Howard Hughes, and this has something to do with national security. I'd like to see Mr. Siegel for a few minutes, tonight if possible."

Someone on the other end covered the mouthpiece, and I could hear muffled voices. Then the talker came back. He gave me the address of a small night club on the Strip and told me to be there at five. I said I would and hung up.

I went to Levy's Grill on Spring, ordered the brisket special and said sweet nothings to Carmen the cashier while I waited for my order. Carmen was looking very ample and busy. Levy's was crowded. I hovered near the register eyeing her, the customers and the candy on the counter. I even bought a box of chocolate babies and popped them in my mouth for an appetizer as we talked between customers.

"How about wrestling next Tuesday?" I said.

"I don't think I'll feel like wrestling next Tuesday," she said without looking at me, as she checked the total on the tab before her. The little guy who handed her the check counted off bills without looking at her or me.

''I meant we'd go to the East side and watch them,'' I explained.

''I know what you mean,'' she said, glancing at me with her soft cow eyes. ''Where have you been?''

''Busy,'' I said. ''Big cases, lots of money. Fame, fortune. I met Basil Rathbone today.''

''You didn't!'' she said, always impressed by movie stars.

''I did,'' I said.

''Next Tuesday?'' she said. I leaned forward with a pleased nod.

''Dinner and wrestling,'' I said.

''All right,'' she said. ''Now leave me alone and stop trying to look down my dress. I've got a job.''

Feeling better, I ate the brisket special, left a big tip and gave Carmen a smile when I paid my bill. Then I headed for the Strip and Bugsy Siegel.

A black Caddy pulled into traffic behind me with two guys in it. Maybe I was being followed. Maybe I was just jumpy. I decided not to take a chance, so I circled the block twice, and they were gone. At least I thought they were gone, but as I later discovered, even a sharp-eyed investigator like Toby Peters makes mistakes.

CHAPTER SEVEN

I was driving slowly down Hollywood Boulevard with an hour to kill when the hour decided it might prefer to kill me. The black Caddy showed up three cars back in the bright sunlight, sending a mirror of buildings and trees back at me and hiding the faces of the two guys in the front seat.

Instead of turning on Sunset I went down Santa Monica Boulevard, picking up Sunset in Beverly Hills and going south toward U.C.L.A. I had an idea of going to Rathbone's house in Bel Air, but changed my mind. I didn't know who the guys behind me were, and I didn't want to lead them to Rathbone. He could think a good case, but I don't know how he'd handle the pair behind me.

I had a few thoughts about who they might be. They might be cops, but I knew enough about cops to know they didn't drive Caddys and they didn't assign two men to tail a private detective about a simple—well, not so simple—murder. They could have been the murderers, which was a more likely possibility since Frye had already tried to kill me. Maybe he had friends who were taking up his unfinished job. It would have been nice to have a little talk with them, if that were the case, and find out what they thought I knew, but I didn't think friends of Frye would be the talking kind.

There was another possibility. They might have been a pair of Bugsy Siegel's boys. Norma Forney could have told him about me. He knew I was coming to see him. Maybe he had something to hide about that night at Howard Hughes'; in which case, the gentlemen in the car behind could still want to act more than talk.

Whoever they were, I decided to try to lose them. We had a merry chase. At first I tried to make it look as if I were simply driving around randomly, but my pair of circles around the block at Levy's Restaurant must have given them the idea that I was on to them.

They stayed close, so I headed for an area I knew—or thought I knew. I went south on Sepulveda past the university, trying to put a little distance between my '34 Buick and their '40 Cadillac by going twelve miles an hour over the speed limit for a residential area. It was almost hopeless. When I got within two blocks of my old habitat, now a recently demolished motel-like bungalow, I hit the floorboard and darted past a cement truck that let a blast out of its horn. With the truck between me and the Caddy and a half block between us, I made a blind turn over the curb and into the lot where I had once lived. It was a mess of rubble and rain puddles. The Buick landed hard and something clanked in the trunk. I remembered the groceries and hoped the milk bottle would hold up under the punishment.

With a sharp right and squealing tires, I spun in back

of a dump truck on the lot. It was full of what looked like my old house, which surprised me because I didn't think my old house had enough material to fill a bicycle basket.

A couple of gloved workmen heaving debris into the truck stopped to glare at me. I willed them to look somewhere else, but it didn't matter. The guys in the Caddy must have seen me. They came flying over the same curb I had hit and came down even harder. I put my car in gear with my foot on the brake and gave it a little gas. The Caddy stormed toward the truck, almost hitting one of the workmen, who jumped for his life, abandoning a window frame which came down on top of the Caddy with a thud.

As the Caddy rounded the dump truck, I went to the other side, tearing my Buick for all it was worth, which was probably about fifty bucks, toward Sepulveda. I hit a rain-filled rut, knocked a sink into the sky and barely missed the cement truck that was turning into the lot I was leaving. I headed back north.

The Caddy driver had trouble turning. I could see him in my rear view mirror, trying to make up the ground he had lost. I was well up the street, pounding the steering wheel with the palms of my hands to urge it on to greater effort.

I caught a yellow light at Wilshire with a Red Top Cab between me and the Caddy. I went through the yellow. The cabbie decided to stop. The Caddy plowed into him and I slowed down to turn right at the next corner and lose myself in side streets.

In spite of the car chase, I got to the Sunset address about ten minutes early. Instead of going right in, I found a sandwich joint with a telephone and called Sergeant Steve Seidman.

"Seidman," I said, hearing someone in the background screaming: "It ain't fair, it ain't fair."

"Speak up," he said loudly. "We have a customer here who feels he isn't being given proper treatment."

"O.K.," I said. "What can you give me on Bugsy Siegel?"

The pause was long and "It-ain't-fair" kept on until there was a sharp crack and then it was quiet.

"Siegel got something to do with the guy we found in your office this morning?" Seidman asked.

"I don't know," I said. "Maybe. Maybe not. Can you give me something on him to work with?"

"I'm going to have to tell *him*," said Seidman. "He's off for the night, but I'll have to give it to him in the morning."

"Fair enough," I said. I held on while Seidman left the phone and turned to find a young woman in a thin coat waiting impatiently for the telephone. She shifted her legs and her coat opened, revealing a tight green sequined gown that caught the light from a Falstaff beer sign. I figured she was a show girl from one of the places on the Strip. She figured I should mind my own business and gave me a look that said so.

Seidman returned to the phone. "I'll give you the highlights," he said. "The file's a few inches thick. Let's see . . .born Williamsburg district of Brooklyn, February 28, 1906. Moved from small stuff to heading an east side gang, combination of Italians and Jews, stuck mostly with the Jews. Arrested in 1928 for carrying a concealed weapon. Married to Esta Krakower. . .let's see. . . . He and Meyer Lansky headed a gang that gave Bugs his name because he wasn't afraid of anything and the other gangs thought he was a little crazy. By the way, he doesn't like to be called Bugs, which is why we continue to call him Bugs.''

Miss Show Business of 1939 tapped her foot impatiently behind me as if she were about to go into a routine. I imagined her breaking into song, throwing off her coat, leaping on the counter and stepping into the soup of a customer. Seidman went on.

''Feud with the Irving 'Waxey' Gordon mob. Lots of shooting. Siegel was almost killed a few times. One time a bomb was dropped on a meeting, and Bugsy got hit in the head by the roof, which contributed further to his 'Bugsy' image. Chief triggerman was a nutty little monkey named Abe 'Twist' Reles.''

''I've heard the name,'' I said. Miss Show Business showed me her wrist watch. I admired it and smiled.

''Siegel came to Los Angeles five years ago. New York cops thought he had been sent here by the mob as a West Coast agent. We think he did it on his own. Likes to be seen with celebrities, good friend of George Raft. He lives at 250 Delfern. Classy neighborhood. Has the homes of Sonia Henie, Bonita Granville, Anita Louise and Norman Taurog. Siegel's house is full of secret panels and rooms. Built them with the place, probably to dive if anyone takes another shot at him. He has unlisted phone numbers which I can't give you.''

''I've already got them,'' I said.

''I won't ask how,'' sighed Seidman. ''It-ain't-fair'' had started up again slow, but was rising to the challenge.

Seidman turned away from the phone and shouted, ''Keep that guy quiet'' He continued, ''Siegel's a health nut—boxing, running. Thinks he's a real beauty. Even talks about going into the movies, but he has a big problem. He was indicted almost a year ago for the murder of Harry 'Big Greenie' Greenberg, a former friend who he and we thought was going to put the finger on Siegel. Case was so–so. Siegel didn't pull the trigger himself, but we had enough to lock him up in October last year. He got out in December when the new DA, Dockweiler, decided there wasn't a case against him.''

''Will you get your ass off that phone?'' squealed Miss Show Business in my ear, breaking the illusion of culture and charm she had worked so hard to build up.

''Sure,'' I said to her. ''Where would you like me to put it?''

''Hey,'' grunted Seidman, ''I've got other things to do.''

''Go on,'' I said, turning my back on Show Business, who kicked me in the calf and stamped out of the place. I held back a groan and listened to Seidman.

''Well, a few months ago, the New York D.A. got his triggerman Reles in a corner and he was ready to turn states and pin the Greenie murder on Siegel. Then. . . .''

''Reles took a dive,'' I said, remembering the story.

''Right,'' said Seidman, ''Shortly after seven in the morning on the 12th of last month, Reles, who had been guarded around the clock by eighteen cops in the Half Moon Hotel at Coney Island, was found dead on a roof extension six floors below his room. The window of the room was open, and from it dangled a makeshift escape line made from knotted sheets and wire long enough to reach the room on the floor below."

"But. . . ."

"But," Seidman continued, "the body was so far from the makeshift line that it had clearly been thrown and had not fallen. Reles had no reason to run. He was supposedly in the safest place in the world for him."

"You mean the cops killed him?" I said.

"I didn't say that," Seidman added quickly. "Someone killed him. They've got another guy in the hole who says he worked with Siegel on the Greenie killing, name's Allie Tannenbaum. Case comes up in a few months, but Tannenbaum won't be enough to convict Siegel. That's all I can give you without an hour or two of reading, and I have a disgruntled taxpayer behind me who needs my attention. Take care, Peters. Siegel isn't a good guy to play games with."

I said I'd take care and hung up. Outside, the strip wasn't really crowded yet. It was still too early for that.

The Hollywood Lounge had both an awning and a doorman, which was what you needed to be a recognized joint on the strip. The doorman looked at me lazily and polished a button on his grey uniform. Inside the door was darkness and music from a juke box. Harry James was blowing "You Made Me Love You." I listened for a few seconds while my eyes adjusted to the interior browns. I started to make out shapes and tables. There was a small platform for a floor show, a bar with a bartender and a dozen or so tables. A man and a woman were drinking and smoking at the bar. Four men were sitting at one of the tables, talking in low tones. At a table near the stage a woman sat alone. It was Miss Show

Business with the sharp shoes. She saw me across the empty room and it was hostility at second sight. I put my hands up in a sign of peace and moved to the bar. The barkeep, a wheelbarrow of a man with enormous bags under his eyes, moved to take my order.

"Mr. Siegel's expecting me," I said softly. "Name's Peters."

The barkeep grunted and waddled to the end of the bar where he picked up a phone, said something into it and nodded at the response. Miss Show Business looked darts at me. I smiled back. Her darts softened and in another few seconds they might have turned to smiles, but I didn't get the few seconds.

The barkeep nodded at a door a few feet away from me. I said thanks, wondering what his voice was like, and went through the door. I found myself in a small hallway facing a narrow flight of stairs. As I started up, I became aware of someone standing at the top and it was a big someone. I was constantly running into big someones.

This big someone waited till I got to the top step and then made a sign with his hands that it would be nice if I raised my arms. I raised my arms and he searched me. Our eyes met and I didn't like what I saw in his. He nodded me through a door and closed it behind me.

The room was a large office with the desk off in the corner as if space had been cleared in the middle for something. Next to the desk stood an ape of a man in a light grey suit with big lapels. Behind the desk sat a guy with even white teeth and a false smile.

The smiler, I decided, was Bugsy Siegel. He was a well-built man with a prominent nose which had taken a break and veered to the left. His dark hair was parted evenly on the left and was receding slightly. His suit was dark and his tie blue. He had a neat handkerchief in his pocket. I suddenly recognized his face.

''You Peters?'' said Siegel, getting up and letting the smile drop slightly. The touch of Brooklyn was still in his voice.

''Yeah,'' I said.

''I know you from somewhere,'' he said suspiciously.

''The YMCA,'' I said.

He snapped his fingers and looked at the ape next to him. The ape was sweating and didn't respond.

''Right,'' Siegel said easing up, ''you work out there too. We never really met.''

''Right,'' I said with a smile at my fellow Y member. I had seen him working out occasionally at the Y for the last few years. We never talked and I hadn't known who he was—the two guys who watched him while he worked out didn't promote friendliness. The guy I recognized as Siegel did a lot of running and swimming, and I had seen him boxing a few times.

''You're not here to challenge me to four or five rounds, are you?'' he said amiably, looking at the ape to appeciate his joke. The ape did so with a small smile. I appreciated his joke too.

''No challenge of any kind,'' I said. ''I need some help. I told you on the phone I'm working for Howard Hughes. On the night of the party you went to at his house in Mirador, someone tried to steal Hughes' plans for some important military weapons.''

Siegel got up quickly from behind his desk. Ape didn't move. Siegel's smile was gone.

"Wait," I said quickly. "I came here for your help. I'm not accusing you of anything."

Siegel nodded cautiously for me to continue.

"At first I wasn't sure if someone had actually tried to steal anything that night," I said, looking at him and trying not to blink and look nervous. "But last night a guy named Frye tried to kill me to stop the investigation and got himself strangled. And this afternoon Major Barton, who was at the party, caught two bullets in his heart before he could tell me anything."

"I didn't like Barton," said Siegel. "You know why I didn't like him?" I said I didn't know and Siegel went on, "Because he knew who I was and said something that didn't please me. He had a few too many belts of booze in him and said things people shouldn't say."

"That won't do you any good if the cops start putting things together and find out you knew him," I said, to keep Siegel talking. "They've got reasons for trying to nail you, and you've got one indictment on your head now."

"You know a lot about my business," Siegel said suspiciously, coming around the desk and stepping toward me. The ape didn't move a muscle, just stood there, sweating.

"Not enough to get me in trouble," I said quickly. "My only interest is in finding out who tried to get those plans and, maybe, who put away two people in the last eighteen hours. They're probably the same person and they're probably up to something that won't be good for this country."

I hoped patriotism would move Siegel or at least back him away from suspicion toward me. It did.

This country has given me some rough times,'' he said. ''But it's given me a lot too.''

You mean you've taken a lot, I thought to myself, resisting the almost overwhelming urge to say it aloud. I was proud of my restraint.

''You know what that Hitler bastard is doing to Jews?'' he said.

I said I had some idea, and he said I didn't.

''If there's a war,'' he said earnestly, ''I'm going to do what I can to help beat Hitler. I was going to tell Hughes that, but his party broke up early and I never got the chance. You can tell him for me.''

''I will,'' I said. ''Now about Major Barton. . . .''

''If the cops try to hang that on me, they'll be wasting their time. I didn't do it. In my business, we only kill each other.''

Siegel calmed himself by taking a deep breath and looking at his well-scrubbed hands. Then he answered the phone that was ringing on his desk. He listened for a few seconds. ''Carbo? All right,'' he turned to me. ''I've got to go downstairs for a few minutes. Talk to Jerry and make yourself a drink if you want.'' Siegel went out the same door I had come through. I looked at the ape named Jerry and he looked at me. I moved to a chair in the corner and sat down.

''Worked for Mr. Siegel long?'' I tried.

''A month,'' Jerry said in a surprisingly high voice. ''And I don't work for him the way you think. I'm a teacher, ballroom dancing.''

I started to smile at Jerry's joke and held back the smile because he wasn't smiling back. I also realized that the reason the furniture was in a corner and Jerry was sweating might give some support to his crazy tale.

''No kidding?'' I said.

''I like dancing,'' Jerry said defiantly, taking a step toward me.

''So do I,'' I said, hoping he wasn't going to ask me to dance.

''I know what you're thinking,'' Jerry said. ''You're thinking a guy that spends most of his time fox trotting, waltzing, rhumbaing must be some kind of a fairy, right?''

''No, never entered my mind.''

Jerry's move toward me wasn't exactly ungraceful.

''I can clean and jerk two fifty,'' he said. ''I'm in a baseball league that plays two nights a week, year around.''

I wondered what position he played but didn't have time to ask.

''You think you can do that?'' he said. ''You think a fairy can lift two fifty and play baseball?''

I couldn't see any reason why not, but I said I saw his point.

''People think a dance teacher walks around on his tiptoes and has a limp wrist,'' he went on. ''Nobody thinks Fred Astaire is a fairy.''

I didn't know and didn't care, but I told him he was right. At that point Siegel returned with Miss Show Business behind him. Her coat was gone, and she spangled and glittered like a dime store.

''Peters, this is Verna,'' Siegel said. ''She's in the lounge show. I'm taking a few dance lessons, advanced stuff from Jerry, and Verna's helping out.''

"Pleased to meet you, Verna," I said, wondering what I had wandered into.

"Listen," Siegel said, coming over to me, "I've got big friends in this town. I know a Countess, a real one, society people, show business, you know. If I can help, let me know. Anything I can do. I didn't see anything at Hughes' that night. I don't know anything. If you want me to, I'll ask some questions, but I don't think this is exactly the kind of thing my people would know about. Know what I mean?"

I said I knew, and he put a hand on my shoulder to guide me out. He stopped at the office door, looked back at Verna and Jerry at the other side of the room. Jerry was demonstrating a step to Verna, who was having trouble understanding.

"You look like an honest guy, Peters," Siegel whispered. "Tell me. You think I'm losing my hair?"

I looked at his hair, and he looked like he was losing it. I said no he wasn't losing it and I wished I had as fine a crop as he. Siegel patted my shoulder, smiled and opened the door. I walked out and shared the small hallway with the guy who had gone over me for the gun.

"Remember," said Siegel. "You need help—you know where to come."

"Right," I said. "Thanks."

The door closed, and I eased my way past the muscle and went down the stairs, feeling his eyes on me.

My father's watch told me it was two-forty-five. My body told me time was running out, and the doorman of the Hollywood Lounge told me it was almost 7:30. I decided to believe the doorman. I had four and a half hours till my meeting with Hughes, and I decided to spend a few of those hours at the Y, urging my body toward a few more years of abuse. The sky rumbled a rain warning.

I drove to the Y on Hope Street, showed my card to the night man, and went down the stairs to the locker room.

The locker door bounced, banged and vibrated, adding a familiar sound to the equally familiar smell of sweat, chlorine and urine and the sight of peeling walls, narrow wooden benches and bare 40-watt bulbs. It was a comforting jazz of light and sound for a confused Toby Peters. I absorbed it with all of my still intact senses as I hung my jacket on the hook and began to take off my shirt.

The sound of running shower water off in the shower room echoed with indistinguishable voices as I slowly undressed and changed into shorts, T-shirt, jock, socks and shoes. A dozen lockers down, a tall kid with sloping shoulders sat in a wringing wet T-shirt and panted heavily. The kid pushed his moist hair back but seemed too tired to reach up and open his locker. I adjusted my soiled supporter, frayed from overwashing in the sink. My shorts were slightly torn at the crotch, my T-shirt was crumpled, sweat-dry and a little stiff, and my gym shoes were worn tennis-flat and giving away at the seams. I savored my socks. They were new, soft and absorbant.

I took a last look at the tall kid and moved down the row of lockers toward the stairs leading to the gym. I was aware of moving, shuffling bodies even before I got to the gym floor. When I came up from the stairway darkness, I faced a volleyball game with five people on each side, all men. The server was a stocky young guy with a white shirt. I turned away from them and headed for the light bag in the corner. I banged away on it for about ten minutes with my handball gloves, softening the gloves and working up a slight sweat. Leaving the plop of the volleyball behind me, I went up the stairs and did a mile on the track.

I was feeling good and not thinking. I made my way to the handball courts and struck it lucky. Dana Hodgdon, a proctologist who was about sixty, was alone on a court. He was a thin guy with white hair which he kept out of his eyes by wearing a sweat band on his forehead.

He was already dripping with sweat when I knocked at the door and asked if he wanted a game. He said sure and after I got a few whacks at the ball, he served. My palms started to swell as they always did. I was feeling great and only lost the first game 21–14. My legs felt good, and my hands were in control of the ball. Some days everything felt right, and I could put the ball where I wanted it. Other days, I could strain and concentrate, relax and forget, change my style and still blow easy shots. In four years of playing, I had only beaten Doc Hodgdon twice. Both games were on the same day and I just barely won. Then he disappeared for a month. When he came back he explained that he had played that day with double pneumonia and a temperature of 102.

Hodgdon played the angles and never moved more than he had to. He played it smart. I played it frenzied and ran myself into exhaustion. I sometimes wondered what was in it for him to play against me, since I was the only one who got a lot of exercise and had anything to gain from a victory.

With my mind pleasantly blank, I went for a low shot

and hit the wall head on. It had happened before, but that didn't make it any better.

Flat on my back on the cool wooden floor, my eyes looked up at the open space high on the rear wall of the court, where people could watch the game or wait their turn. The face of a skeleton looked down at me, attached to a lean, powerful, dark-suited body. I tried to sit up but fell back, dazed.

"How you feeling?" Doc Hodgdon asked, helping me up. I had trouble standing, and Doc helped me off the court and down to the locker room, where I surveyed the damage to my forehead in a shower room mirror. It was slightly swollen, matching the lump on the back of my head. My eyes looked bewildered. Reflected in the mirror, I could see Doc Hodgdon bouncing his handball.

"It feels all right," I said, running cold water into my cupped hands. I brought my face down to the hands.

"Sure you're O.K.?" asked Doc.

"Fine. All right. Go on back, I think I'll call it a night, Doc. Thanks for the game."

Doc turned, and as I examined myself in the mirror again, I saw him pull off his sweat-stained shirt and watched the crescent-shaped scar low on his back disappear as he left the shower room. The rushing sound of water soothed my eyes, and the smell of sweat satisfied my senses—the compensations of a wounded athlete.

I took my T-shirt off carefully to avoid the sudden dizziness that might drop me to the floor, and was about to move to the showers when I decided to take a last look at my head. The mirror had clouded with steam, and as I wiped it clean I saw the image of the cadaverous man who had been in the gallery over the handball court.

His arms were folded and he stared at me with a slight smile.

I tried to ignore him, but a shudder ran through me as if an ice cream cone had touched my bare flesh. I hurried to the shower, where I stood slump-shouldered, letting warm soothing water hit my many scars. More alert, but still heavy-legged, I picked up my shoes, jock, socks and shoes and returned to my locker, where I pulled out my towel and began to dry myself. I dressed slowly, and as I finished I sensed someone behind me. Before I turned, I knew it was the cadaverous man with the deep, dark eyes. He was about five feet away, and I glanced at him. He was wearing a dark suit with no tie. He was over six feet tall. He was nearly bald, and the cadaverous impression of his face was partly a result of this and partly his sunken eyes and a nose smashed almost as flat as my own. The man leaned against a locker, his arms folded, and spoke in a whisper. I didn't like the German accent.

''Please come with me quietly.''

It was more than a request and I tried to figure the man. Maybe he didn't have anything to do with the Hughes case and the two bodies. Maybe he was a determined homosexual, a strong-arm thief, or simply a lunatic who liked scaring people. The neighborhood around the Y was a grab bag of slums and wealth, sanity and insanity. My eyes took in the locker room. It was empty. I turned to stand face to face with the man. A bench stood between us.

''What's up?'' I said, stalling until I could think of something to do.

''Nothing,'' said the man. ''We simply want to talk to you quietly about the events of the last day or so.'' I looked around for the rest of the "we" and saw no one till the man in black allowed his jacket to open enough to show an equally black holster with a large gun.

I devised a brilliant plan on the spot and threw my gym clothes in the guy's face. Shoes, shorts, handball gloves, a lock and a roll of tape hit him, and I turned and ran along the edge of the lockers down two rows. I stopped, looking and listening for possible help. My heart was doing a rhumba that Jerry the dancer would have been proud of.

I could hear the cadaverous man coming down the other aisle. One of the tall lockers near me was partly open. It was narrow, but by ducking slightly and pulling my shoulders together, I squeezed in and pulled the door closed. The metal locker floor gave slightly under my weight.

My pursuer stopped and listened. Footsteps raced around the row of lockers, and I knew the man had heard the locker close. I held my breath as I listened to him make his way down, opening lockers one at a time. Through the slit in the locker door, I watched the man work his way toward me. I had no more than a few seconds before the skeleton with the gun would open the door.

I waited till he was outside my locker and then pushed on the door as hard as I could. Both the door and my body hit the man, sending him backwards over the wooden bench. I was definitely not working myself into his good graces.

I scrambled up and ran through a fire exit in the corner. No one was outside as I headed for the mesh fence that surrounded the tennis courts behind the gym. A drizzle had started. The courts were empty and still wet from yesterday's rain. I leaped for the fence, clinging as my feet missed the links and dropped to the asphalt court surface just as the man arrived behind me. Instead of following over the fence, he raced for the entrance to the courts about thirty yards away. It was the only way out, and I was too tired to beat him to it. I thought of going back over the fence and turned to give it a hell of a try, but going over the first time on top of my workout had taken too much out of me. Ten years earlier, I would have made it. I was almost to the top on pure stubbornness when I felt the pull at my leg. I looked around in the drizzle for someone to call, but there was no one in sight.

I tumbled back into the court and fell into a shallow puddle. The man hovered over me looking casually toward the Y and the street, as if he were enjoying an outing on a clear day. He was smiling a friendly smile as he helped me up and brushed water from my clothes. He kept one hand on his gun under his jacket and I was convinced he could get it out quickly. I didn't like his smile.

"Very quietly," he whispered. "Move very slowly and ask no questions."

There was no point in fighting. The man put an arm around my shoulder and led me slowly back toward and around to the front of the Y. We passed a girl with a book over her head to keep off the rain, but I didn't say anything. There was nothing she could do to help.

He led me to the big black Caddy that had chased me earlier. The front grill was bent from where it had hit the cab. He opened the back door and motioned me in. I went and he slid next to me. A thick-necked gorilla in the front seat drove off.

I thought I might catch my breath, regain some strength and go out the door at the first traffic light if there were enough people around. We turned down Pico and came to a red light in about three minutes. I tried to pull the lock button up, but it didn't move. The man with the skeleton face didn't even turn his head.

For a few seconds, I considered that I might be dreaming, that I had suffered a concussion and passed out on the gym floor or in the locker room. Young Doctor Parry had warned me about further blows to the head, and I was already two above the limit. Maybe I was back in Cincinnati and these were friends of Koko the Clown.

A solid gun in my side convinced me that I wasn't dreaming and the skeleton man said softly, "Don't try anything more. And be very quiet."

We drove out of the drizzle and through Topanga Canyon. In about fifteen minutes we were in Ventura County, and after another twenty minutes we turned into a driveway in Calabasas. I didn't like it, especially the fact that I hadn't been blindfolded. These gentlemen weren't worried about my seeing where I was being taken, which led me to the conclusion that I might not be coming back from this trip.

CHAPTER EIGHT

I could think of a few dozen things I didn't like about the situation, not the least of which was the fact that the two dark-suited gentlemen who were my hosts began to speak to each other in German as they led me into an isolated house on an isolated hill. The skeleton man's gun was out now, and my chance for a run was down to nothing. The gun was a big bulky Luger that could make a big bulky hole in a man, woman, child or tree.

The house itself was badly lit even with the lights turned on. Some of the furniture was covered with sheets, as if the owners were on a vacation. I was led to a wooden chair in the living room and told to sit down. I did. The skeleton man hovered over me with his gun while the short man with the neck muscles and a decided wheeze tied my hands behind me. He was good at it.

There appeared to be some Germanic debate between the two about how to handle me. I was pulling for the wheezer in spite of what he had done to my wrists. I had the distinct feeling that the smiling corpse did not like me, though I couldn't remember having met him before. I was sure I would have remembered.

Skeleton won the debate and the wheezer walked to a radio on a table and turned it on loud. He found *Mr. District Attorney* just as Harrington was telling Miss Miller that he was worried about the D.A. Skeleton didn't seem to like *Mr. District Attorney*. He told the wheezer something in German. The wheezer found some music and turned it up loud.

"Mr. Peters," said the skeleton, turning to me, "we have some questions for you to answer. If you answer them, we have no trouble and we take you back home with a minimum of pain."

He was a clever one. I had to hand him that. He wasn't telling me I would get off scot free if I talked. He figured I wouldn't buy that. His hope was that I'd settle for a little abuse in exchange for freedom and not think about the likelihood of the abuse being eternal.

"There are some things I can tell you," I said. "And some things I can't. I've got a client." I also figured that if I told them everything that I would no longer be needed. I wasn't even sure of what "everything" was.

"We'll start with what you can tell us, then," said the skeleton man to the music of Guy Lombardo. Skeleton man was putting on a pair of gloves. "Before we begin, however, I'd like to know if you have any problems, illnesses we have to be careful of. We don't want you to pass out before you give us what we need. You understand?"

We exchanged professional grins and I said I understood. I played Br'er Rabbit and told him I had ulcers. I had no ulcers. I also had no desire to be hit in the stomach, but considering the state of my head, I tried to steer him to my midsection. As useless as my head had been, it might still have a function in the future if I ever got there.

Skeleton hit me hard in the stomach to the accompaniment of Guy Lombardo playing "Happy Days are Here Again." My satisfaction at having tricked the skeleton was tempered by the pain in my stomach and the taste of nausea in my mouth.

"I thought you wanted me awake," I gasped.

"But I hit you so gently, Mr. Peters. Now, tell us why you killed Frye, the man in your office last night. We'll start with that."

"I didn't kill him," I said. "He tried to kill me and someone killed him after he knocked me out. That's the truth."

"Suppose you go over everything that happened," he said, nodding to the man at the radio to run the volume down so he could hear me. "You must believe that we did not want Mr. Frye to kill you. He was, how do you say it, overzealous. We simply wanted to frighten you a bit. Please believe me."

"I believe you," I gasped, swallowing. Then I told him what happened the night before, leaving out the visit by Trudi Gurstwald and leaving out Hughes. When I got to the point about Frye's message in blood and said he had written "unkind," Fritz-the-skeleton looked puzzled, but Hans at the radio had an inspiration and started to babble something. Skeleton told him to be quiet.

"That was very good, Mr. Peters," said Skeleton. "Now suppose you tell us how much you have found out in your quest to discover who supposedly stole some of Mr. Howard Hughes' military plans. Yes, we know about that."

"I can't tell you any more," I said, looking straight up at him. There was a little more I could tell him. I could have told him about the holes in Major Barton's chest, assuming he hadn't put them there. I could have told him about Bugsy Siegel. I didn't think it meant much, but I decided not to tell him in the hope that stalling would keep me alive long enough to work something out.

Skeleton put his gloved hands together and shook his head sadly. "Mr. Peters," he said. "We can easily cut your insides out so the birds can carry them home to their young. Would you like that?"

"You have a way with words," I said, and he hit me again in the stomach. It was bad. If I had a bleeding ulcer, it would have been worse. Which gave me an idea. I bit the inside of my cheek hard. It hurt like hell, battling the ache in my stomach for the pain championship. I tasted blood, leaned forward and spit a red mass at Skeleton's feet. He danced back quickly.

"Ulcer, bleeding," I gasped and pretended to pass out.

I rolled my eyes back instantly and held them, looking somewhere into the top of my skull. Skeleton lifted my head by the hair and forced my right eye open. Since I was looking into my skull, I couldn't see him, but my blank eye seemed to convince him I was out and bleeding internally from a ruptured ulcer.

The boys had a discussion in German, and I waited while they decided whether to kill me or keep me for a while. I was betting on their keeping me, since I hadn't told them anything much yet. I was counting on them expecting a terrified man with internal injuries who would gladly talk to keep from further pain. The blood from my cut cheek dribbled down my partly open mouth. I was giving them the best show I could.

The radio went off, and I felt myself being dragged across the floor, one man on each arm. It didn't do my wrists any good, but at least they weren't dragging me by the feet and bumping my head.

A door opened and I felt myself thrown into a room. My chest hit something hard and I bounced into what I decided was a bed. My hands were tied tight behind me and hurting.

Hans and Fritz said something more in German and closed and locked a door. I opened my eyes to darkness and listened. They talked more and then I heard footsteps going out the front door and the faint slam of a car door.

From the other room, I heard the radio come on again, and whoever was left in there caught the end of *District Attorney*. My guess was that the listener was the wheezer and that Skeleton had gone somewhere to get or give instructions or buy himself some carryout ribs. Since wheezer seemed to have no knowledge of English, I wondered what the attraction of *Mr. District Attorney* might be.

One thing was in my favor: they were sure I was unconscious and badly hurt. I knew I was awake and hurt, but not as badly as I was half the months of a given year. It took about five minutes to work my way off the bed without making too much noise. The radio helped cover me while the rusty springs did their best to give me away. I crawled under the bed with my face in the dusty carpet.

I swallowed some blood to keep from sneezing and felt around for a sharp spring. I found one and as quietly as I could, ripped the cloth away to give it more room. Then I slowly worked the ropes against the sharp point of the spring. I went strand by strand on one spot, hoping I'd get through before Hans decided to take a look at me. I figured he'd at least listen through to the end of the show, which was just about what it took me to get the rope frayed enough so I could give it a tug and come free.

I had trouble getting my hands back in front of me and convincing the blood to recirculate. I was numb from the shoulders down, and it took about three minutes before there was any feeling in my arms and hands. I crawled out from under the bed and tested my legs just as Jay Joyston was saying, "And it shall be my duty as district attorney, not only to prosecute to the limit of the law all persons accused of crimes perpetrated within this country, but to defend with equal vigor the rights and privileges of all its citizens."

I got behind the door just as the radio was clicked off. Heavy footsteps came toward me. I felt for a weapon and found a lamp on a table near the bed. The door came open and Hans the short wheezer stepped in. He flipped a wall switch and the light came bright in my hand. I gave it a pull, sending the room back into darkness and lunged, hitting him in the face with the base of the lamp. He staggered back into the living room and I came out, dropping the lamp. He was sitting on the floor, stunned, holding his bloody nose and groping for something under his jacket. I ran across the room and kicked at his stomach. His hands came up and he let out a loud "oooph," which suited me just fine. When he turned to avoid any other attack, his head hit the side of an end table and he was out.

I touched my torn cheek and rubbed my sore belly while I did some wheezing myself. I could have waited for the Skeleton to come back and try to surprise him, or I could have called the cops; but the only charge I could use was assault, and I didn't think I could make that stick. I also didn't think I could get the Skeleton to talk, and I wasn't sure of what I could get out of the wheezer when he got up.

I decided to get the hell out of there. I went toward the front door and heard a car pulling up, so I turned and went through the house and found the back door. I opened it just as I heard the front door open and Skeleton's voice hiss something in German. The hiss did more to scare me than a good shout. I ran for the dark and the trees and turned when I got behind a bush about fifty yards away.

In the back door against the light, I could see the Skeleton standing with his pistol and staring into the night. "I underestimated you," he said, "but I won't the next time."

"Who's writing your dialogue?" I said unable to resist. "Monogram?"

He fired a shot in the general direction of my voice, but it didn't come within ten yards. At least I didn't think it did.

I scrambled down the hill in the general direction of where I thought the road might be. I could hear Fritz the skeleton breaking bushes behind me. It was dark enough to hide, but the evening's exercise had taken a lot out of me. I also knew from my experience at the Y how persistent a tracker Fritz could be. He didn't seem to know the area very well, which gave me a good start, but I soon saw that he had an advantage, a flashlight. He may have picked it up back in the kitchen or had it in his coat pocket. Wherever it came from, it sent out a firm beam I could see back over my shoulder.

He seemed to gain a little ground on me, and with the beam extending his distance about thirty yards I didn't want it and a bullet to hit me. I went behind a tree, trying to keep from panting. The tree broke the beam, which fell on both sides of me and then moved away. I could hear the skeleton's footsteps on the other side of the tree. A bug about the size of a quarter decided to nest in my mouth. I spit him out reflexively.

"I hear you, Peters," said Fritz. "And be assured I will find you."

It was confident talk for a man I could now hear walking in the wrong direction, away from me. I didn't give a damn about the road anymore. I moved as quietly and as fast as I could in the opposite direction of his footsteps.

It was about twenty-five minutes later that I finally stumbled on the main road and found a gas station with a wash room. I cleaned myself up, after paying the kid attendant five bucks and telling him I had an accident. I don't know what the kid believed.

The gas station clock said it was 10:30. My watch said it was 4:15. I called Shelly Minck at home, told him where I was and asked him to come and get me. It took some arguing with his wife, but he finally agreed.

I gave the kid another five and told him I'd wait in his toilet till my doctor came for me. I described Shelly and told the kid to tell no one else I was there. He agreed, and I sat there waiting.

Shelly arrived in about 45 minutes, during which time I had stopped the bleeding in my mouth and had come up with no great ideas other than to be careful, have another talk with Gurstwald and talk to the only one present at the Hughes house that night who I had not seen—the butler, Martin Schell. I also had an appointment with Hughes at midnight and would have to hurry if I wanted to come even close to making it.

I let Shelly talk and complain all the way back to L.A. and my parked car on Hope Street near the Y. He talked of ships and shoes and ceiling wax, or at least he talked of cavities and made a bad sex joke about a dentist who seduced one of his patients and got sued for filling the wrong cavity.

He wondered why I didn't laugh. I told him I had a lot on my mind and a sore in my mouth.

"You pay Jeremy to get the office cleaned up?" I asked as he let me off at my car.

"He wasn't around today," Shelly said and then added, "How about writing Dr. Sheldon S. Minck, Specialist, on the new door?"

"Sounds great," I said. "It'll bring in a classier set of clients from the hall."

He pushed his glasses back and nodded in agreement. I thanked him and he pulled off.

I got in my Buick fast and drove for a block without thinking about where I was going. Hans and Fritz had followed me to the Y. They may have known where my car was. They could have been waiting for me to come back to it. The Skeleton of Calabasas knew where my office was and wouldn't have any trouble finding where I lived. He could pick his own time and place, and next time he wouldn't give me a chance to get away.

I drove home, parking my car almost two blocks away on a side street in the hope of getting in through the back door. I almost made it. If Mrs. Plaut hadn't turned on the kitchen light when I hit the alley, I wouldn't have seen the Skeleton standing in what had been shadows a fraction of a second earlier. He backed away from the window into new darkness, and I went back down the alley, sure that he hadn't seen me.

I drove to Culver City as fast as I could and rang Anne's door bell. She answered, and I hurried up the stairs and down the hall. She was about to close the door when she saw my bloody shirt, tired eyes and puffed face.

"Why here?" she said. "Why here?"

"There wasn't anyplace else," I lied. I could have gone to Shelly's or any of a dozen former clients.

Anne was in a robe, and I had obviously gotten her out of bed.

"Come in and make it fast," she said.

I went in.

"You wouldn't happen to have a clean man's shirt around, would you?" I asked, heading for the bathroom. I noticed that the bookmark in *The Keys of the Kingdom* was in about the same place as it had been the last time I was there. "You know, maybe Ralph dropped one or something."

I recleaned my face and took off my shirt. She met me in the bathroom with a clean white shirt. I had been joking, and the joke had turned on me.

"Thanks," I said.

She shrugged and I put on the shirt. It was all right in the chest and sleeves but the neck was too large, which didn't matter since I left it open.

"Does this have something to do with the job for Mr. Hughes?" she asked.

"Yes," I said. "And you got me the job."

"Don't try to make me feel guilty, Toby," she said quietly. "If it wasn't this job, it would be another one."

"You're right," I said. "What time do you have?"

She told me it was a half hour past midnight. As I moved past her, my arm brushed against her breasts. She backed away as if I had bitten her.

I finished buttoning my shirt and went for the phone. I dialed the police and put on my Italian accent.

"Hey," I said sleepily, "They'sa guy in backa the house behind me standing ina the yard with a greata big gun. Yeh. Right now. I got up getta myself a glass milk and I see him there and I say so to Rosa my wife. I wake her up an I say I'm gonna calla cops. So, I'm call." I gave the cop the address, told him my name was Henry Armetta, and hung up.

"Thanks Anne," I said.

"I don't care if you have a bullet in your head next time," she said evenly. "If you come here again, you don't get in."

"Right," I said seriously. "I understand."

I went out in the hall with the sound of the door closing behind me and wondered what I would pull the next time I wanted to see her. It was getting harder all the time.

By the time I got to the address Hughes had told me to meet him at, it was well after one in the morning. I recognized the place as an old movie studio that went back to the early silents. Since then it had been rented out for independents. It was a big barn of a building with a couple of small offices. I went into the outer glass-enclosed office and could see beyond it that the lights were on in the building. A blackboard inside the office had "Caddo Corp" written in chalk. Behind the desk sat one of the two FBI look-a-likes from my first visit with Hughes. The other one stood next to the desk.

"You're late," said the one behind the desk as he rose.

"I was detained," I said.

"Mr. Hughes said to tell you that your services were no longer needed," said the other guy. "You will be paid for two weeks work with a bonus. Mr. Hughes insists that people be prompt to appointments."

"Let me get this straight," I said, pointing at the last one who had spoken. "I'm getting fired from this case because I'm an hour late?"

"It's not quite like that," said one of the two without emotion.

"Is Hughes in there?" I asked evenly.

"Yes," Number One said, "but he doesn't wish to see you."

"He'll see me," I said. "Since I took this job for Mr. Hughes, I've been beaten, brained, tortured and shot at. I've had two corpses dumped on me and my life might not be worth a used Hughes drill bit. Now I'm late this morning because of this case and I'm going to see Howard Hughes or make a lot of noise."

Number One came around the desk and reached for my arm. His plan was to push it behind my back and shove me out or further. He was prepared for me to struggle, but I didn't. I wasn't after a fight. I was after his gun. I let him take my left hand and reached for the gun under his jacket with my right. It came out easily. Number One dropped my arm and backed away. I levelled the gun at him.

"I'll see if I can find Mr. Hughes," he said, making a move to the door. Number Two slowly showed his empty hands.

"I've got a better idea," I said. "Why don't we have him come here?"

I turned the gun to the ceiling and fired a couple of shots. The gun jerked in my hand and made a hell of a noise in the small room, sending my eardrums quivering.

In less than ten seconds, Howard Hughes burst through the door leading into the studio. His mustache was gone, and he was wearing a fedora tilted back on his head. He had no jacket and looked even younger than before. A group of people stood behind him including a guy in a cowboy suit. Hughes looked at my gun without a sign of concern and waved away the people behind him. He closed the door and faced me, saying nothing.

"I'll say it slow and I'll say it once," I said. "I've got a lot to tell you, but the most important thing is that I'm late tonight because two guys who I think had something to do with taking those plans kidnapped me and beat the hell out of me. I should be dead now or collecting pats on the back for getting here at all instead of having this bunch of shit about being fired for being late."

Hughes put up his hand calmingly.

"O.K.," he said. "You're right. You're back on the job. I'm sorry."

I believed him and put the gun on the desk.

The two guardians of the gate moved forward toward me, but Hughes stopped them.

"I said I was sorry," he said. "I mean it. My word means something."

The two backed off, and I told them to take better care of their weapons in the future. I had not made two friends.

Hughes motioned to me, and we walked into the studio and through a crowd of people, one of them a young man in a cowboy suit. They parted, and Hughes went toward a set with me at his side.

"I'll get the details from you in a few minutes. We're shooting some scenes for a Billy the Kid movie," he explained. "But that damn Mayer is trying to beat us with a Billy the Kid of his own with Robert Taylor. I'll need a new title for mine."

"How about 'The Outlaw?' " I suggested.

"Sounds too much like a gangster picture, "Hughes said." I already did a gangster picture, *Scarface*. I don't want people to get confused. I'll think of something. We'll talk after this scene."

Hughes moved away from me into the lights, where he looked as uncomfortable as a man could look. The kid with the cowboy suit came over to Hughes, who talked to him softly. Then a girl joined them. She was dark and pretty and had an enormous rising chest.

I turned to ask someone who she was and what was going on, but I was being shunned like an M.G.M. spy, probably because of the shooting incident and the weary madness in my face.

After a few minutes of talk, Hughes moved out of the lights and left the girl and the kid on the set, which looked like an old stable. He called softly for the camera to roll, and someone shouted "Quiet." Hughes motioned for action, and the guy with the sticks appeared and clapped them, announcing it was "Take ten on scene five."

The kid took a step toward the camera with the heaving bosom of the dark girl behind him. His guns were drawn and he said to the camera, "Waal Doc, you borrowed from me; now I borrowed your gal."

And Hughes called "Cut."

"Good job Jane, Jack," Hughes said. "That's enough for tonight." Then he had a brief conference with a young man with a clipboard and moved to me.

"It's quieter to shoot at night," he explained, leading me off into the studio away from the crew and cast as they broke up for the night or morning.

I didn't care one way or the other, but I didn't say anything. The studio looked big enough to house the late, great Dirigible Hindenburg. We sat down on a couple of coils of rope and I told him my tale in detail. He listened carefully, asking me to repeat once in a while, and I remembered to keep my voice up so he could hear.

"Looks like I was right, doesn't it?" he said.

"Looks like something's wrong," I said.

"What do you want to do next?" Hughes asked.

"How about setting up another dinner party for Saturday night? Same guests plus me, minus, of course, Major Barton. I'll try to pull something together by then, and it'll be interesting to see if anyone turns you down."

"And if they turn me down?" he said.

"I think I know someone who can persuade them to change their minds," I said. "Oh, another thing. I need photographs of everyone in your house that night, guests, servants, everyone."

"I'll get them," said Hughes. "Keep me informed and take care of yourself."

"I'll try," I said. "Sorry about the scene in the office."

"You were right," he said and turned away to talk to a man with a clipboard, who was waiting patiently about twenty-five yards away.

I lifted my weary body from the coil of rope, walked across the studio and through the office without looking at the two guards, and stepped into the predawn darkness.

The radio kept me company on the way home and told me that the Pacific Parleys were expected to collapse and that frenzied troops were still fleeing the Reds near Rostov. It sounded like a tongue twister and I tried repeating "Fleeing the Reds near Rostov" ten times fast. Just as I pulled up a few blocks from my house, the radio told me that a 23-year-old girl named Velma Atwood, a carhop, had shot herself because her boyfriend had been drafted.

It was the end to a perfect day. I counted on the cops having checked out my complaint and the Skeleton calling it a night. To be safe, I took the .38 from my glove compartment and dropped it in my pocket. Then I opened the trunk. My groceries were all over the place, but nothing, including the bottle of milk, was broken. I stuffed them back in the brown bag and went home. Nobody was waiting for me this time when I let myself into Mrs. Plaut's and made it up the stairs to my room. There was no one in my room. To play it somewhat safe, I didn't turn on the light, and put the groceries away and undressed in the dark. For over a month, I had been sleeping on a thin mattress on the floor to cut down on my back pain. The problem was that when I fell asleep I automatically turned on my side or stomach, which was no good for my back at all. That night I pulled the mattress into a corner, placed my .38 within reach and lay with my head propped on a pillow so I could see the door.

Sleep had almost taken me when I thought I heard something at the door. I tried to shake myself awake, but it felt like I was making my way through five layers of cotton candy.

The door popped open and a long thin shadow speared its way into the room followed by a definitely Germanic, "Mr. Peters?"

I almost shot my first man. The gun came up, and I tried to level it, expecting him to shoot me first and grateful that he had been dumb enough to frame himself in a lighted doorway while I was in the dark.

The cotton candy feeling gave me just enough hesitation, so as it turned out, I didn't shoot Gunther Wherthman. Even if I had taken a shot at him I would have aimed a foot over his less than four feet in height. But considering the fact that I am not a particularly good shot and hadn't fired a gun in years, I might have missed what I was aiming at and hit Gunther in a vital part. It was a sobering thought.

So, "What's up Gunther?" I said soberly, "besides you and me."

"I am sorry to have startled you, Toby," he said as

precisely as usual, ''but I thought I heard you in here and was sure you would like to know about the events that took place a short time ago.''

''Cops came,'' I said, sitting up. My back felt all right, but my stomach hurt like the Huns at Rostov. ''Chased a guy away and came in here asking questions?''

''Precisely,'' said Gunther. ''There was a shot fired. The police asked if we knew an Italian neighbor named Armetta. I'm afraid Mrs. Plaut provided them with no solace or information.''

''Come in, Gunther,'' I said. ''And leave the door open. I don't want to turn on the lights.''

Gunther came in. I could see now that he was properly dressed in a robe with a sash and slippers. In contrast, I was wearing a pair of undershorts and a torn YMCA shirt with a hole in the navel.

''Does the man in the yard relate to your spy inquiry?'' asked Gunther.

''Right,'' I said. ''Have a seat, Gunther.''

He climbed up on a wooden chair near the table, and I got up to heat some water for tea. Gunther preferred tea to coffee and I didn't want coffee to keep me awake.

I told Gunther about my most recent exploits and the fact that I seemed to be running into a hell of a lot of Germans in Los Angeles. He explained that there was a colony of German refugees from Hitler in Los Angeles and that it was growing all the time.

''Most of them arrive in New York,'' he explained, ''and move as far away from Europe as they can. Hence, Los Angeles.''

''Well, I have some hard evidence that what they ran from might have followed them clear across the forty-eight states.''

We drank our tea and I got hungry, so I fumbled in the dark and opened the can of pork and beans I had bought that day. Gunther politely accepted a cup of pork and beans and I ate the rest out of the pot, trying to avoid my torn cheek.

''If it will be of any help,'' he said, wiping his mouth with my last paper napkin, ''I will make some inquiries among my clients for whom I am translating, on the chance that they will recognize the cadaverous man and the man with the wheeze whom you encountered.''

''I'd appreciate that,'' I said.

Gunther thanked me for the snack and said goodnight. I cleaned the dishes and settled back in bed.

In a few minutes, I was asleep. If I dreamed, I don't remember it.

CHAPTER NINE

Breakfast consisted of a very slowly eaten bowl of Kellogg's corn flakes and a glass of milk with Bosco syrup. The pain in my cheek where I had bitten off more than I wanted to chew had not subsided during the night and made eating unpleasant. My stomach and head were still sore, and the hint of humidity in the air threatened my back. In short, it was a typical morning for Toby Peters.

While I was brushing my teeth with my finger and Doctor Lyon's tooth powder, Mrs. Plaut knocked and came in without waiting for an invitation. She began padding around the room.

"Mr. Peelers, you should have seen. Police and shooting. We could have used your comfort. Little Mister Wherthman says you are a private police officer. It's a comfort to have you here when there's trouble, a comfort, but you weren't here."

She stared at me peevishly.

"I'm sorry," I said innocently, rinsing my mouth and wincing at the pain. "What happened?"

"You should have been here," she repeated and left the room. The phone rang and I raced Mrs. Plaut for it. I was handicapped by a sore stomach, but I beat her by half a length, despite her one-length lead. Breathing hard I said, "Hello."

"Toby," came the familiar voice of my only sibling, "get to my office fast. Now. Don't go for a walk. Don't see a client. Don't have breakfast."

"I already ate."

He hung up.

No one tried to kill me when I walked outside, which gave me renewed hope. So, full of confidence and with almost a half bottle of Jeris Hair Tonic on my head, I dodged the marathon rope-skipping girls, who had moved to the sidewalk, and headed down the street toward my car. Behind me I could hear their melodious young voices joyfully chant:

> Rooms for rent; inquire within;
> A lady got put out for drinking gin.
> If she promises to drink no more,
> Here's the key to Barry's door.

I could still hear their giggling half a block away.

I put my .38 back into the glove compartment and in fifteen minutes I was semi-legally parked near Phil's station. I pulled down my visor with the "Glendale Police" card on it. It was old and frayed and I don't think it had ever saved me from a ticket, but it was worth a try.

The squad room was almost empty, a morning emptiness of smokers coughing and bleary eyes of a new shift with too little sleep and an old shift that had been up all night. A cop with his jacket off played with his suspenders while he listened to a fat woman who leaned toward him and croaked, "You woulda done the same. Anybody woulda, wouldn't they?" The cop with the suspenders nodded in boredom and looked toward the squad room door for his relief or the Second Coming.

I knocked at Phil's door and walked in without waiting for an answer. If it was good enough for Mrs. Plaut, by God, it was good enough for me.

Phil was behind his desk with three dark folders lined up neatly in front of him. He was drinking a steaming cup of coffee from a white mug.

"Sit down, Toby," he said evenly. "And listen. Listen quietly before you say a word. You understand?"

I told him I understood and sat down. Phil drank a little more coffee, looked at me, drank more coffee and opened the first folder.

"The gentleman we found in your office yesterday," he began, "was covered with type A blood. His was type B. The gentleman was carrying false identification. His name wasn't Frye. It was Schell, Wolfgang Schell. I know that because the FBI told me. The FBI came to look at his body and papers before we even had him at the morgue. It seems Mr. Schell is an illegal alien, a German with a bad reputation—I don't have enough corpses of my own, the goddamn Nazis have to send me more." Phil had no love for the Germans since they got him almost fatally wounded in his first battle in the big war in 1917.

The look Phil gave me made it clear I was somehow responsible for his present problem with the Germans, and in a way he was right. So, I said nothing. Besides I was learning a lot. Schell was the name of Hughes' butler, the butler Toshiro had described as less than pleasant. But the butler's name was Martin, not Wolfgang.

Phil pulled out a pile of photographs from one of the files on his desk and shuffled through them. He went through them quickly and finally stopped at one that made him bite his lip. He held it up for me to see. It was a black-and-white picture of the message written in blood. It still looked like he had written ''unkind'' to me.

''What the hell does this mean?'' Phil asked, almost crushing his still hot coffee cup in his big fist. ''Was the Nazi nuts, or was he leaving some information?''

''I don't know,'' I said as Phil replaced the photo.

''You're in good company for a change,'' he said. ''The FBI doesn't either. Think you might tell me where you were yesterday between about noon and two?''

He was about as disarming as a charging rhino.

''Having lunch with Rathbone,'' I said. ''Why?''

''Guy named Barton, Air Force major got a few bullets in his pump out in Westwood,'' Phil said, staring at me.

''So?'' I said blankly.

''So, Schell, the dead Nazi in your dental chair had Barton's phone number in his wallet. Schell knew Barton, and they both wind up dead on the same day, and you discover one of the bodies.''

''So,'' I said.

''So,'' said Phil standing up, ''the call to report Barton's death came from a guy with a phony Italian accent. Do we know anybody who likes phony Italian accents?''

I shrugged.

''More coincidences,'' Phil said, turning to the third folder. ''Early this morning we got another call from someone with a phony Italian accent, complaining about a prowler with a gun. The prowler happened to be in your back yard, and the Italian gave a phony name. More coincidence?''

''You are one hell of a good cop, Phil,'' I said seriously.

''Maybe you're just one hell of a poor private detective,'' he came back. ''Ever think of that?''

''What happened to the prowler?'' I asked, trying to change the subject.

''Got away. Took a few shots at the cops who came to check. One of the cops said he got a glimpse of the guy. Looked like Dracula. You know anyone like that?''

I said I didn't. Phil put his hand to his face and pinched the bridge of his nose as if he were getting a headache. He suffered from migraine headaches. The headaches made him angry, and instead of giving in, he always fought them. A steady stream of coffee always seemed to help when a headache was coming, and a steady stream of me always seemed to make it worse.

''You don't intend to tell me anything, do you, Toby?''

''I don't know anything, Phil. Honest to God, I don't know anything.''

He looked at me evenly before he threw the file of photographs in my face and reached over the desk for me. I backed away just in time. Phil's headache had slowed him down. The problem was that even though it slowed him down, it made him more determined. He came around the desk and I backed up to the wall.

''The FBI on my back,'' he whispered through gritted teeth. ''The Air Force on my back. Mysterious messages from Nazi corpses. And you.''

No sound of rushing feet came from outside. It seemed they were used to people being thrown around Phil's office. Having been thrown around Phil's office several times before, I decided not to let him hit me without some return fire this time. It might just provoke him even more, but sometimes a man has to put his back to the wall and stand up for what he believes. This wasn't one of those times, though; I was just tired of getting clobbered.

Phil stopped a few inches in front of me. A blue vein throbbed in his forehead. I was fascinated. He stopped dead.

"Get out," he said, pinching the bridge of his nose.

I collected the file and its contents from the floor and put it on his desk, pocketing the photograph of the message in blood.

"Phil," I said, looking at his back. "I'm sorry, if . . ."

"Just get the hell out of here. I'll probably find your corpse somewhere in the next few days, and that'll just add to my work load."

A few more cops and robbers were in the squad room. It still smelled of sweat and coffee. The fat lady was telling her tale to a young uniformed cop, who listened attentively. Seidman was in a corner talking to a tall, skinny guy who kept nodding in agreement. I left, feeling pleased with myself that I had gotten something to work on.

I made phone calls from the Rexall Drug Store near the station and marked each one in my Hughes expense book. The first call was to Dean at Hughes' Romaine office. I told him Hughes owed me for two more days work. He said he'd have it delivered to my office. Then

I called Bugsy Siegel. After I convinced a guy with marbles in his mouth that Siegel knew me, he gave me the phone number of a gas station on Sunset where I could reach him. I called the station, and a guy named Moll answered. He got Siegel to the phone.

"It's me, Peters," I said. "You said you'd help if I had a problem. I've got a problem. I want everyone who was at Hughes' party last week to be there again on Saturday at eight. Some of them might not want to come."

"And you want to be sure they're there, right?"

"Right," I said.

"I already got my invitation from Hughes this morning," Siegel said. "Give me the list, and I guarantee they'll all be there."

I pulled the list from my pocket and read the names and addresses to him, omitting the now deceased Major Barton. I also thought Hughes was one efficient son-of-a-bitch to get invitations out so fast.

"I'll call Rathbone," I said. "I'm sure he'll come. I'm worried mostly about the Gurstwalds and your friend Norma Forney."

I was also worried about Siegel, but I let that pass.

"The krauts will be there," Siegel said amiably. "So will Norma. Anything else?"

"No," I said.

He hung up. Then I called Rathbone and asked if he wanted to take a ride out to Mirador with me to talk to Schell, the butler. He said he would, so I headed to Bel Air to pick him up after taking a look at the photograph of the word in blood. It got me nowhere. My reasons for taking Rathbone were more than just to satisfy his curiosity. I figured that with him at my side, Sheriff Nelson and Alex the Deputy might be less inclined to lynch me, which is why I also agreed to let Rathbone take his car and drive.

He talked about his new Holmes movie script, and I brought him up to date on the case including my trip to Calabasas, the identification of the corpse in the dental chair, and the fact that Barton knew that corpse. I also told him about the FBI's interest.

''Curious,'' said Rathbone, who was wearing a dark suit and a white sweater. ''If your skeletal friend is to be believed, he and his cohorts did not murder the man in the chair and probably did not murder Major Barton.''

''Maybe,'' I said, playing my tongue against my raw cheek. ''Then who did and why? I'm grinding up bodies, but I don't know if I'm getting any closer to finding out who killed anybody or who, if anybody, took Hughes' plans.''

''And so,'' he said, ''out of frustration, you set up a little gathering of suspects for Saturday night in the hope that something will happen.''

''Like Holmes,'' I said, watching the telephone poles flit by.

''No,'' said Rathbone, ''you, like so many others, have not read the Holmes stories. Holmes did not gather the suspects. That, I think, was a creation of the American theater which Conan Doyle deplored. It is a bit of bravura and vanity which would not have been beyond Holmes, but would probably have struck him as ungentlemanly, though it is sometimes difficult to penetrate that persona so carelessly created.''

We were nearing Mirador and the turnoff. I told Rathbone about Sheriff Nelson, and he suggested I slouch down even more. I slouched, and Rathbone drove evenly down the wide main street of Mirador. Alex wasn't at his post in the window. The yellow police Ford wasn't in front of the station. The car door still lay in the middle of the road, but there was no cat or kid. I sat up and Rathbone drove down the road, past the Gurstwald's and into the Hughes' driveway.

The Mirador police car was there. I sighed and led Rathbone to the front door. Toshiro answered.

"Good to see you Peters, Mr. Rathbone. You came just in time for a problem," he said seriously.

He turned and led us down a corridor to a big paneled door, which he slid open. It was a billiard room pretty much like any billiard room you see in the movies except for the sheriff and the deputy at the table and the corpse in the butler's uniform lying on his back on the green cloth. I knew it was a corpse by the open eyes and the knife in his chest. That didn't surprise me. I was used to corpses, even ones with open eyes and knives in their chest. I wasn't even surprised by the fact that the corpse was wearing a butler's uniform. What did surprise me was the fact that I recognized the corpse on the table. He was the skeleton who had taken me for a ride to Calabasas.

"Come right in, Mr. Peters," Nelson said, glancing at Rathbone, whom he recognized. "Mr. Rathbone? Sir, a pleasure to meet you, even under such circumstances."

Rathbone took his hand and looked at the corpse.

Nelson looked at the corpse as if he were trying to line up a double rail shot but didn't know how to do it with this obstacle. Alex just stood looking at us.

"We seem to have Mirador's first murder in a decade," Nelson said with a false grin. He looked scared and confused. He was a man who didn't know what to do with a corpse.

"Last murder we had was back in 1930," he said, avoiding the immediate problem. "Wife hit her husband with a rock down at the beach after a party."

I looked at the body.

"Victim's name is Schell," said Nelson. "Martin Schell, part-time butler here. Case looks pretty simple."

"How is that, Sheriff?" said Rathbone with sincerity.

"Only two people in the house," he said. "Cook is in a drunken heap in his room. Jap here," he said nodding at Toshiro, "is still standing. He must have done in the butler. Fight or something."

"If I killed him," Toshiro said reasonably, "why would I call you?"

"Cover yourself," he said. "Happens all the time."

"I thought your last murder was in 1930," I said. "That's not all the time."

"With apologies to Mr. Rathbone here," Nelson said, removing his straw hat and mopping his brow, "I'm gonna have to tell you to keep your remarks to yourself, Peters. I might start asking you questions about this."

"Sorry," I said, "I've got an alibi. I just drove in from Los Angeles with Mr. Rathbone."

"I wasn't accusing you," he said peevishly, "just checking all the possibilities."

"Well you might start by calling the State police," I suggested. "The longer that corpse lies there, the tougher it's going to be to get any information from it. I assume you are going to call the State police to handle this, or were you going to take it on your own?"

"I was just about to have Alex call them when you came in," Nelson said nervously. "Alex, find a phone and call the State police. Tell them there's a murder here. Tell them. . . ."

"I know what to tell them," Alex said with what might have been sarcasm. He started to leave the room.

"And take this Jap with you and keep an eye on him," Nelson said, looking at Toshiro. "The troopers are going to want to talk to him."

Toshiro shrugged and accompanied Alex out of the billiard room. Rathbone circled the table, examining the corpse and the floor. Nelson warned him, not knowing what else to do.

"This house is full of exits," said Rathbone. "A side entrance, rear entrance, garden entrance." He opened a door in a corner and looked in the room beyond. "There's an open door leading down to the beach. I'd guess our Mr. Schell had an assignation here with someone. He assumed the house would be relatively deserted except for the cook and chauffeur. There is no sign of a struggle, so apparently he had no fear of his murderer and anticipated nothing.

"I'll bet the Jap did it," said Nelson.

"Well, if he did," said Rathbone," he changed his clothes before calling you. Look at the knife. Whoever plunged it in hit a main artery. Blood spurted out. See the lines of blood on the handle. Might not have been a great deal of it, but certainly a spray would have hit the assailant. The young man who was just in here is certainly dry and there are no stains on him. You might check his room, but I'm inclined to think he was telling the truth. His point was well taken. Why call you with evidence so clearly against him coupled with a quite reasonable assessment of the present prevailing anti-Japanese sentiment in this country?"

"He was being clever," said Nelson, "trying to throw us off."

"There is," said Rathbone, "such a thing as being so clever that one is stupid. Whatever he may be, the calm young man who just left here is not stupid. However, there's no reason to debate the issue, sheriff. We can leave that for the State police."

"What was Toshiro's story?" I threw in.

Nelson looked at me with distaste, but Rathbone's show of attentiveness changed his mind, and he talked, keeping his back to the corpse.

"Said he heard someone going out the door in the other room," Nelson said. "Didn't see anyone. Then he came in here, saw the corpse and called us. Said it didn't take him more than three minutes to get to the phone. We got here five minutes later, about two or three minutes before you came in."

Over Nelson's shoulder, I nodded to Rathbone, indicating that I wanted to get out of the room. He took the cue with a lift of his chin and said, "Toby, would you go out in the car and get my cigarette case? I seem to have forgotten it." Before Nelson could raise a protest, Rathbone went on, "Sheriff, you might want to step over here and have a look at this."

I hurried out of the room and found my way to the servants' quarters. I didn't run into Alex and Toshiro, but I went past the room where the cook, Nuss, was sleeping in the same position I had seen him in 24 hours earlier. I found the room Toshiro had told me was Schell's and went in fast. I didn't find much, but I did find a photograph of Schell and the man who had been found strangled in Shelly's dental chair, the man who Phil said was Wolfgang Schell. I put the picture in my pocket and hurried back to the billiard room. If I had it figured right, two brothers named Schell and a Major named Barton had been killed by hands unknown in the last few days. Whoever the killer was, he believed in variety: one strangling, one shooting, one stabbing.

When the State police arrived a half hour later, they found a silent gathering in the billiard room. The cop in charge was a beefy pro named Bill Horrigan, who asked Nelson what he had touched and told us all to get out of the room while his men went over it. We went out. An hour later, Rathbone and I were headed back to Los Angeles in his car.

"We've had a busy murderer," I said.

"I don't think so," said Rathbone, pulling into a roadside restaurant called Jason's. "I mean it's quite likely we have more than one murderer involved here."

"Which will simply complicate my life further," I said.

Over a steak sandwich, Rathbone explained:

"Murder Number One in your office was a strangling. The killer did not have a gun and was apparently quite strong. Strong enough to take a bullet and still strangle the unfortunate Mr. Schell. Victim Number Two, Major Barton, was shot cleanly through the heart, while Victim Number Three on the billiard table was stabbed in rage by someone who knew him."

"Too much," I said, sinking my teeth into fat and meat. "You work it out your way and I'll go mine, with my feet and a big mouth, which reminds me."

I excused myself and made a call to Dean at the Romaine Office and told him about the corpse at Hughes' house. Knowing Hughes' love of secrecy and his contacts, I thought he might want to set his machinery going to keep Hughes' name out of it. Dean said thanks and hung up.

Rathbone drove me back to his house and my car, wished me luck and said he'd see me on Saturday at Hughes' house. Then I drove back to my rooming house. I didn't feel like facing Shelly yet, and I didn't think I had anything to fear at home. The skeleton, Schell, who was looking for me was dead. What I had to do fast was put the puzzle together. Phil would probably see a report on the second dead Schell, make some inquiries, find out about my being at the Hughes house and call me back for a talk.

The rope-skippers were gone when I pulled up and Mrs. Plaut, seated on her porch swing, greeted me with a hearty "Hello Tony."

I waved back and tried to step past her.

"A lady called you," she said, reaching out to hold me with a bony hand. "Very bad English. Said her name was Judy, but you shouldn't call her."

"Thanks," I said, figuring she meant Trudi Gurstwald.

"Did you hear about the shooting here last night?" she said, moving her arm to let me pass.

"Yes," I said. "You told me this morning."

"Oh yes," she remembered, "I told you this morning."

I made it up the stairs and into my room. In the next room, I could hear Gunther and someone with a high voice arguing in German. I tried to put it from my mind while I pulled the two photographs out of my pocket. I flattened the Schell Brothers and thumbtacked them to my wall. They were a somber pair. I didn't like the fact that the picture reminded me of the photograph in my office of Phil and me. I thumbtacked the second photograph of the word in blood next to it and took off my shoes.

I got on the floor on my mattress to take the weight off my back, touched my sore cheek with my tongue and stared at the photographs, waiting for them to talk, but they said nothing. The only voices were in German from the next room. Life had been Germanized in the last week and would probably be more so when the war actually came.

There was a knock on the door. The knocker turned out to be one of Hughes' bodyguards. "You asked for these," he said, handing me an envelope.

"Thanks," I said. He left without another word. I opened the envelope and found photographs of everyone who had been at the Hughes party. I spread them on my table.

A few minutes later, there was a slight, tentative knock at the door.

"Come in," I called and looked back over my shoulder. Gunther came in politely.

"Do you have any tea, Toby?" he said. "I have a client and. . ."

"Sure," I said. "You know where it is. Take what you need."

Wherthman was as quiet as he could be, which was pretty damn quiet, but he had trouble finding the tea. He took enough time that his client came to the door.

"Gunther?" a tentative voice asked.

"I'm getting some tea," Gunther said.

"Come on in," I said, staring at the photographs. I just kept waiting for the photographs or my mind to tell me something.

I heard the footsteps of the client come into the room and stop not far from me.

"Here they are," said Gunther.

"Schell!" said the client with a heavy German accent.

I rolled over to face the man. He was staring at the picture of the Schell brothers on my wall.

Gunther Wherthman's client was about my age and height. He wore blue denim trousers and jacket and a white shirt without a tie. In his mouth was a nickel American cigar. He had a two-day growth of beard and wore a pair of rimless glasses on his slightly hooked nose.

"You know them?" I said, rolling over and getting up.

The client looked at me with amusement and nodded.

"Berlin, 1933," he said. "They were brownshirts, Nazis. They arrested me. I have a lump on my back as a souvenir. I hope they are well." The accent was heavy, but I could make out the words.

"They're both dead," I said, "murdered in the last two days."

The client shrugged and pulled on his cigar.

"Don't go away, please," I told the client. "Gunther, why don't you make the tea here?" I pointed to the photographs on the table of everyone who had been at the Hughes' house for the party. Martin Schell's picture was on the top.

"Yes," said the client. "That's him."

"Sit down," I said, offering him one of my three chairs. "How about some cereal?"

He looked with distaste at my Kellogg's carton on the table and said, "We didn't eat that kind of thing in Augsburg."

"We have work, Toby," Gunther said.

"A minute, Gunther," I pleaded.

The client looked at the rest of the spread-out photographs and put his finger on one.

"Ah," he said. "I knew this one too. The three of them were together when they came for me in Berlin. They'd been out enjoying themselves one evening and they continued their entertainment at my expense."

"God sent you," I said, smiling at him.

"I do not believe in God," said the man with some irritation. "I am a Communist, which, by the way, is why I am not in Berlin at the moment. I might also mention that there are, perhaps, thirty or forty Berliners in Los Angeles at the moment who would remember that trio."

"Mister. . . ."

"Brecht," said the client, holding up the photograph. "Bertold Brecht."

"Mr. Brecht," I said. "You may have just solved a murder."

"Humm," he said. "I should like that."

Wherthman poured us all some tea, and Brecht told me his tale about the Schells. His cigar was turning the room into a putrid cloud, but I wanted to hold onto him.

"It wouldn't have taken much to recognize the Schells," said Brecht. "If you lived in Berlin in 1933 and had trouble with the Nazis, you probably met the Schells. Gunther, I'll have to go now. I've enjoyed the tea and the conversation. I'd like you to finish the poems. I've got a young man named Bentley working on the play. Now, Mr. Peters, should you need me further, Gunther has my phone number and my address in Santa Monica."

We shook hands and he left with his hands deep in his pockets.

Gunther and I finished our tea, and Gunther explained that Brecht had been a famous young playwright in Germany. Apparently he had only been in the United States about six months. According to Gunther, he had taken a ship from Russia to San Pedro and settled down a few miles from where he landed.

"He had always been no more than a step or two ahead of the Nazis," said Wherthman.

"He's Jewish?" I asked.

"No, family was Protestant-Catholic. But as he told you, he is a Marxist."

I finished my tea, scratched my stomach and turned to the pictures on the wall.

"Now," I said, "if I can only figure out why Schell wrote 'unkind' on the table in his blood while he was being strangled, I may have most of this sorted out."

Gunther finished his tea and got down from the chair to move to my side. Since his head came just above my belt, he had to look almost straight up to see the photograph.

"That doesn't say 'unkind'," he said to me.

I looked down at him.

"It says 'ein kind'—a child—in German. It isn't English."

Of course, Wolfgang Schell was German. He wouldn't write in English when he was dying. But the new possibility that followed didn't give me a lot of cheer. Had Schell been trying to leave a message that he had been strangled by a child?

CHAPTER TEN

I decided to be unreachable for a few days, just in case Phil put things together faster than I thought he would. Using a semisturdy suitcase given as a fee by a pawnbroker named Hy O'Brien, I packed in a record four minutes, asked Gunther to keep an eye on the room for me and headed into the morning. I made it to my car just in time to have Jimmy Fiddler tell me that Milton Berle had married Joyce Matthews and Ronald Reagan was right behind Erroll Flynn in fan mail at Warner Brothers with Jimmy Cagney a close third. It sounded unlikely to me, and I was about to tell Fiddler so when I felt something cold and hard on my neck.

My guess was that my injuries had caught up with me and the first sign of paralysis had struck. When a short, thick head and little eyes appeared in my rear-view mirror, I breathed a weary sigh. Life seemed to be a never-ending series of attacks punctuated by periods of confusion. This was an attack, and the wheezer had a gun to my neck. His nose was held together by a strip of tape, and his face showed a variety of scars from the lumps I had smashed in his face. Overall, I would have called my work a triumph of cosmetic surgery, but I had the feeling that Wheezer thought otherwise.

"Aross miten zu en leben," he said, or something to that effect. His face looked more confused than angry, and I had a fair idea why. He couldn't speak English.

Since I couldn't speak German, any attempt at conversation seemed pointless without an interpreter. I didn't think Wheezer would want me to head back and get Gunther, but I didn't want conversation to die, or I might follow the example.

"Voss vills du?" I said, heading for Broadway and as much traffic as I could find.

"Give tsu mier du parperen du cameram," he said.

He was sweating, and the Luger in his hand bumped on my neck.

"Certainly," I said, "whatever you say. Wass you . . . oh shit."

"Paperen, cameren," he said again, impatiently looking out of the window to see if anyone was watching. Not being familiar with L.A. and the neighborhood, he didn't know that he probably could have had a horizontal guillotine around my neck, and the chance of anyone paying attention would have been nonexistent, unless a tourist from Delaware happened to have lost his way.

"Pictures, pictures," he said, the sweat dripping from his furrowed brow, and loosening the tape on his nose he blurted out *"Paperen, cameren."*

We were making progress, though we were a long way from Wendell Wilke's One World. Wheezer thought I had some papers, plans, or photographs, probably the stolen Hughes plans, though why he should think I had them was a new mystery.

"Schell," he said.

I thought he was saying the German word for fast, so I pointed to the thick traffic ahead.

"Nicht Schnell!" he bellowed, hitting me on the lump already on my head and almost knocking me out. "Schell. Martin Schell."

The car veered while I tried to make one image out of the vibrating three or four I was seeing. I managed to get them down to a double image. The truck driver I had almost hit leaped out of his cab, tilted his cap back and started for me. Wheezer pointed his Luger at the driver, who promptly returned to his truck and toilets or whatever was in it.

"Take it easy, Hans," I said slowly, hoping to either calm him or get through to him. I did neither. He hit me again. I was more ready for it this time and held the car steadier, but the blood trickling down my neck brought nausea.

"Look," I said, getting angry and desperate, "if you keep *gaspolotzing* me *en kopf,* you'll get *dreck. Farshteh?"*

His face was a confused mask of sweat. He peeled the moist tape from his sweating nose, revealing a cut that must have hit bone and was barely clotting. It should have had a few stitches.

My guess was that Wheezer knew Martin Schell was gone. He thought I had strangled Wolfgang Schell, and he probably figured I had gotten to Martin too, who had been out gunning for me. Apparently Martin had the plans, and Wheezer thought I had done him in and taken them. At least that was the best I could do. His face told me reasoning with him was impossible. I either gave him some plans or he blew my head off. I had the feeling that even if I gave him the plans I didn't have, he would blow my head off. He had already paved the way by chipping a hole in my scalp.

"*Yah, will Ich do,*" I said in resignation, heading for a parking lot. It was an old empty lot where an enterprising owner had put up a small shack to collect a few parking dollars till he could find a sucker who would put up a liquor store and make his fortune. Right now it was just a ten-cent-an-hour lot for about fifty cars, and it was half full. The attendant was a Negro about twenty-five. He wore a clean blue shirt with "Larry" stitched on it in white.

"Twenty-cent minimum," he said, leaning down with his hand out.

Wheezer showed him the gun, and the young man straightened up and said softly, "I ain't about to die over twenty cents. You want to park that bad, go on."

"Humor him," I told the young man.

"Hey," said the young man, "I just work here. I'm not about to die here. Consider him humored."

"*Shah,*" Wheezer said, looking around desperately. I decided the sweat wasn't just from fear. He had a fever. His wounds had probably become infected, and he needed medical treatment.

"*Paperen, paperen,*" he shouted at me.

"*Paperen* him, mister," Larry the attendant suggested, "or he's liable to paper both of us."

A Plymouth pulled in behind us and hit his horn for

us to hurry up and park. This didn't help Wheezer's control of the situation, so he prodded my open wound.

"O.K.," I said, reaching into my jacket carefully to pull out the package of photographs of the people at Hughes' party. "Here."

I handed the packet over my shoulder and watched Wheezer in the rear view mirror. The Plymouth was laying on the horn. Wheezer needed both hands to check the packet. When he tilted the gun hand up to hold the envelope, I slid down in the seat and threw my right elbow at his face. I made contact with his already infected nose and he pulled the trigger as he screamed. The bullet went out the open window and cracked the glass on the little shack a few feet from attendant Larry, who hit the dirt. The Plymouth backed out of the lot fast, and I rolled out of the driver's seat door.

Wheezer came out of the car moaning and holding his bleeding nose with one hand while he tried to level the gun at me. I got to my knees and hit him in the stomach with everything I had. A small crowd gathered across the street and watched us, but a wild shot from Wheezer hit the building above them and sent them running. I went around my Buick with Wheezer in pursuit, got to the street and just missed a bread truck making a turn from Fifth Street. Wheezer was right behind me and not quite as agile. The bread truck hit him and came to a halt at the curb.

I couldn't tell if Wheezer was dead or breathing. He wasn't moving. I staggered back to Larry, who was on his feet now in a not-so-clean blue shirt. Behind us the bread truck driver had run to kneel over Wheezer. Traffic was stopping. I pulled my wallet out and peeled off a five, gave it to Larry, who pulled his eyes from the prone body of the man who had almost killed him.

"Describe me," I said, seeing two of him.

"What?" he said, thinking he had another looney on his hands. Then he understood.

"You're about sixty with white hair," he said. I gave him a ten. "And you're Chinese."

"Right," I said, giving him another five. "And my car?"

"A new blue Caddy," he said.

"You got it," I said and got back in my Buick.

"You better take care of that head," he said, leaning toward me.

"Too late," I said. I could hear a police siren coming up fast. A good size crowd had gathered around Wheezer. I pulled around a row of parked cars and into an alley, traveling in the opposite direction of the lot and the sound of the siren. If Wheezer were alive, I doubted if the police would get anything sensible from him for a long time.

I saw four alley exits in front of me and had to stop till they became one. Then I drove slowly and very carefully to County Hospital.

My Emergency Room credentials were perfect, a bleeding head.

"Take a seat," three fat nurses said. "We'll be with you in a minute."

"Any more than that and I'll need a transfusion," I said. They smiled and I told them it was no joke. They walked away, merging into a single body.

It was a slow Thursday afternoon, and the crowd was down to two: me and a woman holding her stomach and moaning. The woman was about fifty and wearing a white uniform. She was either a nurse, which didn't seem likely, or a Good Humor Man in disguise. I found a washroom and took some paper towels, which I pressed to my throbbing head. When I got back to the waiting room the Good Humor Woman was gone, and the three nurses were there.

"It'll be a few minutes," one said.

"You know I see three of you," I said.

"A few minutes," they insisted.

"That's all right," I said, groaning. "If you see Doctor Parry, you might tell him his uncle is in the Emergency Room waiting."

A few minutes later the hospital loudspeaker lady called for Doctor Parry to go to the Emergency Room, and three minutes later twin Doctor Parrys were in front of me. They were both in their late twenties with thin yellow hair and glasses. They looked tired.

"Well, Mister Peters," Parry said wearily, "what's going on this time?"

"My head this time," I said, pointing at my head.

"I'm not your personal physician, Mister Peters," he said.

"Call me Toby. I thought we were friends."

He blew out air and motioned for me to follow him into a small examining room. I bled my way after him and sat down. He looked into my eyes.

"What do you see?" I said.

"The back of your skull," he said. "Your head is completely empty."

He examined the back of my head none-too-gently.

Outside I could hear an ambulance siren come to a snarling stop.

''Normal people your age don't lie on the sidewalk and hit their heads until they crack,'' he said, prodding away while I made faces. ''Nurse said you made a joke about seeing double.''

''Sometimes triple or quadruple,'' I groaned. ''Right now you look like the Dionne quintuplets.''

I could hear a rush of people in the hall outside the room.

He sewed my scalp and said nothing.

''Aren't you going to warn me?'' I tried to coax him into conversation.

''About what?'' he said. ''You have a natural immunity to warning. In all the time I've been a doctor. . . .'' he began.

''Which isn't too long,'' I added.

''Which isn't too long,'' he agreed, finishing the fifteenth or sixteenth stitch. ''I have never seen as marred and as bruised a specimen as you are. If you survive till next week, I'd consider it a privilege to show your traumatized body at grand rounds. I might even write a paper on you or start a betting pool among the house staff about how long you'll survive. I suppose there's no sense hospitalizing you. You'll just run out and drive some poor nursing station superintendent insane. Sit there a while.''

I watched the wallpaper curl and felt the stitches tighten. He was back in five minutes with a small bottle of pills.

''Take two every few hours and come back to see me on Monday or earlier if it gets worse. I've got to check these stitches.''

"Thanks, Doc," I said, getting up and heading for the sink, where I gulped a couple of pills and dropped the bottle in my pocket.

"Don't thank me, Wyatt," he said sarcastically. "You're a medical curiosity."

He left, and I moved slowly to the door. The room was reasonably steady. When I opened the door, my knees almost dropped me. Sergeant Seidman was standing in the waiting room, talking to the fat nurses, who were now one nurse. Two well-dressed young men were with him, asking questions. I caught part of a question.

"When will we be able to talk to him?"

"Maybe never," she said, which threw a scare in me. I closed the door gently and went through a second door that led to a treatment room, where a nurse and a doctor were working frantically on someone lying on a table. Someone was the Wheezer.

If my brain had been operating at even half mast, I would have realized that Wheezer would have been brought to County.

"Get the hell out of here," a doctor who couldn't have been more than twelve shouted at me.

I eased past him and out the door about ten feet away from Seidman and the guys who I decided must be the FBI. I walked slowly with my back to the bustle of the main part of the hospital. In about five minutes, I had worked my way back to the Emergency Room parking lot and into my car. My knees were shaking. I gobbled four more pills for good luck and worked them down dry.

I drove a few blocks away, parked and took off my

jacket and shirt, changing them for the clean but crumpled shirt and zippered Gabardine jacket in my suitcase.

On Main I found a hotel that had seen better days and parked my car in an enclosed garage, where it wouldn't be spotted easily if my brother started looking.

Complete with suitcase I made it through a jungle of potted palms in the lobby, registered as Melvin Ott, bought a package of Wilbur Buds and a Pepsi and went to my room. I didn't know what time it was. The going over or the pills or both got to me, and I sang myself to sleep with a medley of Russ Columbo songs. I got through "The Devil and the Deep Blue Sea" and was well into "Just One More Chance" on the line which went "I'd want no others if you'd grant me just one more chance," when Koko applauded and pulled me into the inkwell.

CHAPTER ELEVEN

I woke up and found myself looking down at a newly dead man in the bed. His face was white, his head swollen and his nose smashed. It was me. The sensation passed, and I was back in my body with a mouth full of sandy lettuce. There was no phone, and my watch told me it was six, which meant nothing. I found my tooth powder in Hy O'Brien's suitcase. I brushed with my fingers and rinsed, cupping my hand. I was wary of the dirty glass on the sink. I gulped a few more of Dr. Parry's magic pills and shaved with a once-used blade. It wasn't too bad.

The shower didn't work when I turned it on. It just screamed, but that was enough to scare the roach in the tub, who scurried for safety down the drain. I turned on the tub tap and gave the bug a free ride to the ocean and me a bath. The soap said "Elysian Hotel" on it, which was fine except that I was staying at the Hotel Miraflores. I toweled off with a chic towel with a see-through hole, as they might say in a Movietone Newsreel fashion feature.

I hoped I had not slept through to Saturday. It was light out, but my beard with definite grey stubble had told me more than a few hours had pranced by.

When I went down to the lobby, the guy at the desk, who looked something like Nat Pendleton, confirmed that I had slept through Friday and owed him another day's toll. I paid him and found out it was almost noon on Saturday. Making my way through the maze of potted palms in the Miraflores lobby with my suitcase in hand, I found the street, cursed the bright sun and headed for a hot dog stand half way up the block.

"How's the news?" I asked the rail-thin dark waitress behind the counter.

"Roosevelt says he doesn't like the Japs' answer," she coughed, putting down her cigarette. "What'll it be?"

"A transfusion," I said. "If you don't have one, I'll settle for two dogs with grilled onions and the works and a large Pepsi."

She disappeared. The other patrons and I ignored each other, and I brought my expense book for Hughes up to date. I considered listing the payoff to Larry the parking lot attendant as a parking expense, but decided to call it "essential supplementary secrecy," which might appeal to Hughes.

The dogs weren't bad. They weren't good either. I burped politely, got my car out of hock and headed for Mirador.

If you discount the times the back of my stitched head hit the top of the seat, making me groan, the trip was uneventful. My chewed cheek was healing, and I had some hope that the case would soon be ended. I didn't listen to the radio, and I didn't admire the scenery. Instead, I just drove, trying to think and having no luck.

The main street of Mirador was teeming with life. The cat who had sat on the door was walking down the sidewalk. A small boy and girl were drawing in chalk on the street. An old man was sitting on a wooden chair in front of the bait store, and Sheriff Nelson and his deputy Alex were leaning against the yellow police car with their arms folded, chewing on toothpicks and watching me.

I pulled up next to them.

"You're expected up at the Hughes house," Nelson said, anxious to have me gone.

"Troopers find the murderer?" I asked innocently.

Nelson spat toothpick.

"They found nothing," he said, avoiding my eyes. "And they're acting like it never happened. Couple of boys in spanking new suits said they were FBI, stuck their noses in and everything got quiet. I'll bet Hughes pulled his strings and connections."

"I'll bet," I said.

"What happened to your head?" Nelson said, looking at me. "You poke it in one place too many?"

"Something like that," I said. "Well, I'd like to sit and talk to you all day and listen to the crickets, but I've got to get going. Maybe we'll go fishing together some time."

Nelson let out a sick laugh.

"Just get up to your little party and stay as far from me as you can, Mister Private Detective."

I pulled into the wide pebbly street and drove up the road past the Gurstwald's to Hughes' place.

"Well," said Toshiro, answering the door, "it looks

like I'm the butler for tonight. I guess Mr. Hughes got the impression that you wanted no new faces except yours."

"Right," I said, following him in. "Is Hughes here?"

"Waiting for you."

He led me up a flight of stairs to a door. I looked around and there, indeed, as Trudi Gurstwald had said, was the washroom with a good view of Hughes' temporary office. Toshiro knocked. No answer. He knocked again much louder.

"Come in," called Hughes. I went in and Toshiro disappeared, closing the door behind me. I stood at the door and brought Hughes up to date. Hughes didn't look up.

"The FBI has been convinced," Hughes said finally, looking up from the pile of papers on his desk, "that my name should be kept out of the death of the man Schell."

"And that comes first," I said, finding a chair and sitting down without being invited.

"For me it comes first," he said. He was wearing a dark suit and dark tie. The suit looked about two sizes too big for him. He could have stuffed a pillow inside his jacket and played a bizarre Santa Claus.

"Listen Peters, I don't care what the world thinks of me. I do things for myself. Why should I care what the masses think when I don't care what individuals think about me? I've been alone since I was a kid and my parents died. I've been surrounded by people who wanted one thing from me, money. When people know I'm Howard Hughes, they fawn or gawk and I can't live my life."

"So you live it better when you spend most of it creating elaborate ways to hide?'' I said. ''The more you make a thing about secrets and hiding, the more people want to find out your secrets and see what you're hiding. I make my living finding secrets. I've seen it.''

''That's my concern,'' he said placidly.

''Maybe you like being known as the man with secrets,'' I said. ''The man nobody knows.''

Hughes looked at me solemnly.

''What are you so angry about?'' he said.

''Well, maybe I'm a little angry because I have a hole in my head, which I got working for you, and you didn't even notice. Maybe I'm a little angry because three people have been killed in the last few days, probably because of you and your damn stolen plans, and you haven't shown the least bit of interest in any of them.''

Hughes looked at me woodenly. I had shouted loud enough for him to hear clearly.

''In a sense, you're right,'' he finally said. ''But tell me the truth, do you really care about who killed them? One of them apparently tried to kill you. One kidnapped and beat you. The other one, Barton, you didn't even know.''

''I care,'' I said. ''They were human beings, part of the same fraternity I'm in and I think you may be in. If one of us dies by a bullet, a knife or a gun, it shows how easy it is for any of us to go. We have to respect lives, all lives.''

''What about the lives of people who take lives?'' he said with more curiosity than emotion.

''I deal with that when it comes up or leave it to other people,'' I said.

"It's up right now in Europe," he said. "And it will be up in the Pacific in weeks."

"And you care?"

"I don't know," he said. "It interests me. Peters, we're not going to agree on this, so suppose you just tell me what you want done tonight and we'll do it. I respect professionalism. You're a professional. Let's leave it at that."

Hughes was beginning to remind me of a manufactured robot with a little record inside. There was no way of getting inside the shell of the man. He was a walking cliché, but in addition to that cliché he was also a man who knew how to get things done and had the guts to get them done. I gave up.

"I want the murderers," I said. "You want your plans. I think someone did take them, and I have a plan to try to get them back. You go ahead with your dinner party, and after dinner, you and I meet in the hall off the dining room to talk privately. I tell you something and take off, something that gets the murderer to follow me."

"You're convinced whoever took my plans will be at the dinner," he said.

"I'm convinced whoever committed murder will be at the dinner," I corrected.

"How do you know they'll hear you talking to me?"

"Simple," I said. "People have to speak up to you anyway because of your hearing problem. I'll exaggerate a bit."

I half expected him to lay out some protest about his inability to hear, but he didn't.

"I think it's a bad idea," he said. "You might get yourself killed."

"And you'd never find out about your stolen plans."

"I'm not that unfeeling, Mr. Peters," he said. "Now if you'll excuse me, I've got some work to do." He turned to his papers, ending our conversation, and I went out in the hall. I made my way to the billiard room and hit the balls around for about an hour till my head started to throb. I ignored the blood stain in the middle of the green felt. Then I wandered into the kitchen to find Toshiro and Nuss-the-cook. Nuss was awake and reasonably sober. He sang loudly while he cooked, mostly Nelson Eddy songs. I preferred him dead drunk. Toshiro set the dining room table, explaining that Hughes had ordered new dishes and silverware for the night.

"He doesn't like to use dishes other people have used," Toshiro explained. "He said it's unclean."

"If you're Howard Hughes, you can afford new plates every meal," I said.

"Yeah," Toshiro went on setting the table, "but when you have our Nuss as the cook, forget about cleanliness. If Hughes took one look at him working in the kitchen he'd order out for burgers."

At 7:30, the first guests, Norma Forney and Benjamin Siegel, arrived. Norma had on a white dress and black belt, and Bugsy wore a modified tux with a white carnation. He smiled and took my hand after Toshiro let him in.

"Everyone will be here," Siegel said confidently. "Which means the Germans, Gurstwald and his wife. Germans can be tough to convince. Norma was a little tough to convince too."

We had moved into the billiard room, where Siegel began to play like a semipro.

''Ever been in Germany, Mr. Siegel?'' I asked innocently.

''Never,'' he said, lining up a shot.

''You, Miss Forney?''

She looked at me over a drink Toshiro had brought her.

''When I was but a youth,'' she said lightly, ''I went to school in Berlin. I had thoughts of being a doctor, but Hitler came along and I sold a few short stories to the New Yorker and. . .''

The doorbell rang. In a few minutes, Basil Rathbone was escorted into the room. We had ''good evenings'' all around and some pleasant chat until he could get me aside.

I briefed him on everything that happened, including the identification by Gunther Wherthman of the message in blood.

''Of course,'' said Rathbone, ''I should have guessed. Just like *Study in Scarlet,* but there the message in German and in blood was designed to throw the police off the trail. In this case, I think it has more significance. Whatever it means, we can be sure the butler didn't do it. He himself was killed.''

Rathbone's words sent a chill down my back. He had dropped into place the one thing that had confused me. I was certain now who had killed all the three men in three days, and it didn't give me a hell of a lot of pleasure.

The Gurstwalds came last, even though they had the shortest distance to come, no more than half a mile. He was red-faced and silent, giving Siegel glances that should have turned the mobster to ice, but Siegel enjoyed it.

''Good to see you,'' said Siegel, taking Gurstwald's reluctant hand. ''Glad you could make it.''

''I am here under protest,'' Gurstwald fumed. Trudi tugged at his arm to keep him in control. She was wearing a fluffy green dress, a delicate thing that didn't hide the firmness of her body. She stayed near Gurstwald and gave me a warm, friendly greeting.

I offered to get them drinks. He refused, but she said she'd like something mild. I got her something mild while everyone watched Siegel make shots on the table where Martin Schell's body had been stretched out a day ago with a knife in it. Someone in the room had done it, but I couldn't tell from their faces.

Toshiro refilled several glasses and gave me a ''what's up'' look. Trudi pulled herself away from Anton, who had plunked himself down in a corner chair to sulk. Pretending to admire a picture of a dead salmon near my head, she whispered.

''I was worried about you,'' she said. ''What happened to your head?''

''I started the war with Germany early and became one of the first victims,'' I whispered, smiling across the room at Norma Forney. Rathbone had taken up a cue and was playing billiards with Siegel and holding his own.

''I don't understand,'' she said, and the look on her face made it clear she didn't.

''Did you know Barton was dead?'' I said. ''Have you noticed he's not at our little party?''

She looked around.

''They killed him?'' she asked.

''Who?''

"Whoever he was stealing those papers or things for?" she said.

"Maybe," I said. "I think I'll find out tonight."

"Please be careful," she said, touching my shoulder as she turned. It was a good solid touch and reminded me once again what a firm woman she was. She joined her husband, and people started to look at their watches.

About nine, Hughes showed up, looking neat but not comfortable. He gave the group a boyish grin, which he then cut off, and carefully avoided shaking hands. I had noticed that before. Maybe it was part of his plan for staying clean.

Twenty minutes later we were all having dinner. Toshiro served, and Norma Forney did most of the talking, asking questions of Rathbone, who told stories about making *David Copperfield* and *The Adventures of Robin Hood*. He told about his years building his reputation as a Shakespearean actor and the current identity problem he was having with Holmes. He talked about his little daughter Cynthia and did a hell of a good job of putting an impossibly tense group at ease. No one talked about the murders, the plans or the reason for the get-together. Bugsy Siegel told about how he had lost thousands of dollars earlier in the year in an attempt to extract vitamin A from sharks' livers.

Anton Gurstwald said nothing and looked at his plate. Hughes watched whoever spoke with complete attention, but showed no emotion and rarely responded.

After the fruit cup, while Toshiro was clearing the table, I stood up and asked Hughes if I could see him for a moment in the hall. Rathbone had already agreed to talk softly so we could be overheard. I excused myself and Hughes followed me into the hall. I purposely pushed the door so it wouldn't quite close, and it cooperated by swinging back open about half a foot.

"I don't know why he wants me to meet him at midnight," I told Hughes, "but that's the way he wants it. Says it's safer that way."

"It's up to you, Peters," Hughes said, which wasn't much of a line, but it was enough to let me go on.

"His name is Brecht or something like that," I said. "And he says he knew the Schells and has some information, knew them back in Berlin in '33. I don't think it's much, but we don't have much to follow up. I set it up at NBC back in Los Angeles. Rathbone arranged for us to use Studio B so we could be alone. He's afraid of going to a private place."

Logic might have dictated that a radio studio at night in 1941 might be a rather private place, but my murderer didn't know too much about NBC or radio stations.

"Well, good luck," said Hughes. "Sure you don't want one of my men to go with you?"

"I'm sure," I said. "He said I should come alone, and alone I'm going."

The conversation in the dining room had stopped, so it was a good bet they had all heard our little show. I didn't know how Rathbone rated our acting. I thought I was somewhere between a Republic serial and a Universal B feature. Hughes was about high-school theater. If I was right about my killer, that would be good enough.

I drove back to Los Angeles slowly with plenty of time before midnight.

Lowell Thomas said Japan's reply to the U.S. demand for an explanation of troop buildups was "unsatisfactory." The Japanese had said their troop movement was to counter Chinese movements. Thomas gave the odds as 60–40 that we'd be at war with Japan in a few days.

I turned off the radio, leaned over to check on my .38 in the glove compartment and gulped a few more of the magic pills from Dr. Parry. The Hughes party would break up early, according to our plan, to give the killer plenty of time to get to Los Angeles. The possibilities were that the killer would wait outside NBC and try to get Brecht before he came in. Since Brecht was not coming at all, the killer might get tired of waiting and either give up or come in, thinking that Brecht might have gotten past unseen. Another possibility was that the killer wasn't falling for this and I'd spend some cold hours in an NBC studio.

I was confident who the killer was from Brecht's identification of the guest's photo, but I had no evidence. An attempt on my life would probably qualify as pretty good circumstantial evidence, and that would probably be enough to break down the killer's story.

I pulled into the parking lot around 11:30. The tires crunched against the pebbles and sent them pinging inside the fenders, triggering a shock wave through my sore cranium. I considered taking a few more pills but decided against it.

Rathbone had arranged for the side door to be open for me. Security at night, he had said, was nil. A confident grin and a wave could get one past the night guard, and there were plenty of other ways into the building which could be found by an enterprising detective or murderer.

I went in and found my way to Studio B, where I had

watched Rathbone and Nigel Bruce rehearsing for the show they would be doing live on Sunday. I remembered that Sunday would be the next day, and I vowed to listen to the show if I was alive.

While pondering and waiting, I thought about buying Christmas presents for my brother's kids. I wondered what one bought for a two-month-old baby girl.

It was then that the bottom of my foot began to itch. This was followed by the other events with which I began this tale, events which left me standing face-to-face with a killer who was holding a large handgun with a correspondingly large silencer.

CHAPTER TWELVE

I stood among the broken discs of yesterday and today, looking into the barrel of that gun and feeling no satisfaction at having trapped the killer. My curiosity was satiated, but my life, justice and Howard Hughes' peace of mind had very poor prospects at the moment. I was least worried about Howard Hughes' peace of mind and justice.

"Well, what now Trudi?" I said.

She had closed the door, and far off somewhere I could hear the music of a big band, probably Woody Herman, bouncing gaily.

Trudi Gurstwald had changed from her dress to a khaki hiking suit.

"Now," she said softly, "I must kill you."

"A little talk first," I asked, "for the sake of our recent love?"

"I really meant that in your office," she said. "I wasn't trying. . . ."

"I thought you were trying pretty hard, and I'll bet you say that to all the boys, and I mean *all* the boys."

I would have been better off keeping my mouth shut, but a bleeding foot, a sore head and the prospect of death do strange things to a man, if you are willing to consider my membership in the human race.

"I must be quick," she said. "The noise . . ."

"How did you get away from dear old Anton?" I said, trying to keep her talking while I found a weapon. My hand found a box of Kleenex on the table behind me.

"I didn't tell him," she said. "We have separate rooms, and I told him I was sick and wanted to go to sleep. Then I climbed out the window. I've done that several times."

"I know how agile you can be," I said. She didn't smile.

"I used to do a lot of mountain climbing back in Germany," she said.

"I know what a good climber you are too," I continued. My double entendres were going far beyond her but I had the nervous desperation of a third-rate stand-up comic who can't keep the lousy jokes from coming, even though the last customers are walking out on him. "Where did you learn to shoot, and where did you get that gun?"

"I learned to shoot in Germany too. My father was a Field Marshall, and Anton's company manufactures silencers for these guns. Now, I really have to . . ."

The gun came up and leveled at my stomach.

"At least you owe me an explanation," I said, leaning back as unthreateningly as I could. "No one's here but a drunken engineer and an all-night music player."

She thought about it, glanced at her watch, and agreed.

"I didn't want to do any of this," she said. "Schell didn't know I was Anton's wife. He saw me the night of the party. He was there to try to get Hughes' plans. That's why he took the butler job. When he saw me with Anton, he had a better idea. He and his brother Wolfgang knew me before I met Anton. I had run away from home and was working in a . . . a. . . ."

"House?" I tried.

"Yes, a bowdy house. Is that how you say it?"

"Well, I don't but that's close enough."

"I was a young girl. I was stupid. I thought it was fun. Music. And the brownshirts spending money. It was during the Depression in Germany too. That must have been when Brecht saw me. I remember him from his poems and plays. I remember once they arrested him for a poem saying Christ wasn't divine. Maybe that's when he saw me. I don't know. Then when Schell saw me at Hughes' house, he told me I had to get into Hughes' room and take photographs of any papers there. He had tried but couldn't get to them. Hughes had never left them alone. If I didn't, he said, he would tell Anton what I had been. I had nowhere to go, Toby Peters. I couldn't go back to my father in Germany. He wouldn't have me."

I tried to nod sympathetically. As far as I was concerned, she could become Shaharazad and go on till an engineer showed up for work in the morning.

"Well, Schell gave me a small camera. I knew how to use it. I left the party to go up to the bathroom and went into Hughes' room."

"And Major Barton saw you coming out," I tried. "You didn't see him coming out. You pleaded with him not to tell, told him you would explain and promised sweet nothings. How was he in the dental chair?"

''Major Barton drank too much,'' she said softly.

''His loss,'' I consoled.

''You told Schell and gave him the camera with the plans?''

''No,'' she said. ''I kept the camera and told Schell that Barton had gotten it from me. It was the only thing I could think to say to keep it from Schell. I didn't want him to have it. I didn't want it turned over to the Nazis.''

''Very noble of you,'' I said, moving my sore and bloody foot slowly off the sharp point of a black disc on the floor. ''Then I came in investigating everybody at the party, and you knew I would get to Barton soon. So, you got to me first and told me it was you who had seen Barton, not the other way around.''

''Yes,'' she said, ''but you must believe. . . .''

''Lady,'' I said. ''You've got the gun. I'll believe any damn thing you tell me. If you're going to tell me about the wonders of our moment of love, you might prove it by putting that gun away.''

''I can't,'' she said. ''You'd tell.''

''How about if I crossed my heart?''

''How can you keep joking? You are joking, aren't you?''

''I think so,'' I said. ''I can't really analyze what fear does to me. I might even start giggling soon. So, you got to Barton?''

''Yes,'' she went on, dropping her gun slightly. ''He told me that Schell had come to him and demanded the photographs. Schell offered him a price. Barton said he didn't tell him I had the camera.''

''That's why Schell had Barton's phone number in his wallet,'' I added. ''Go on.''

"Barton was thinking of going to the Air Force," she went on, "after you and Mr. Rathbone had been to see him. I arrived at his house when you had left. He was afraid and he had been drinking. I could not appeal to his. . . ."

"Emotions," I supplied.

"Yes," she said, "emotions. So I had to shoot him."

"And Martin Schell?" I said.

"At first he thought you had gotten the camera from Barton. Then he decided I might have the camera and photographs after all, and he told me to come and see him immediately. I was afraid, but I went. I walked over on the beach. It's not far."

"And. . . ." I urged her.

"I told him I didn't have them. He hit me and said I had been no good in Berlin and was no good now, and he was going to tell Anton if I did not give him the photographs. I was going to give them, but his face was so twisted. He hurt me. The knife was his. He had taken it out and put it on the pool playing table to threaten me. I grabbed it and stabbed him hard. I am strong."

"I know," I said.

"I didn't mean any of it," she shrugged. "It just happened. It was *Shiksal.*"

"What?"

"Fate," she said. "That's the English word."

"And Fate is going to make you put a couple of bullets in me? What about Brecht? He'll still talk about having seen you with the Schells, or are you planning to find him and put a few bullets or a knife in him? I have a better idea. Why don't you go to the library and get a Berlin telephone directory from 1933 and start with the

A's and work through the *umlaut*s killing everyone who might have known you?''

''I can only do what I can do,'' she said helplessly. ''If I stop now, Anton finds out. Maybe I go to jail. He would not help if he knew what I had been. No, I must keep going. I'm sorry, Toby Peters.''

''No sorrier than I am, lady,'' I said, deciding on a pitiful leap and the hope of a stray bullet. Even if I was lucky, survived the leap and knocked the gun away, I wasn't sure if I would be able to handle her. She was one tough lady and I was one weak private eye with a half a head and a swollen foot. But what choice did I have?

The question was answered for me by the door flying open and a body leaping into the room. It was a beautiful blur in which a foot licked out, hitting Trudi's hand and sending the gun flying against the wall. I went down covering my head, expecting the gun to discharge and spit out a silent bullet ricocheting around the little room till it stopped in something solid, like my head, which seemed to hold an unaccountable attraction for projectiles.

Trudi turned, and the blur hit her on the side of the neck. She staggered back and would have been painfully pinned on a turntable if I hadn't hurried upright to catch her. Her unconscious weight almost dropped us both to the floor, but I managed to put her down more or less gently and hobble to the now harmless Luger in the corner.

''You were just in time,'' I said.

''No,'' said Toshiro. ''I was listening at the door. I

could have come in much sooner. I've been watching you since you got here."

I looked at Trudi, whose neck was at a clearly uncomfortable angle. I turned her head and her face went limp.

"To what do I owe this last minute rescue?" I said, sitting on the table in the corner and ministering to my sore leg.

"Curiosity and perhaps a touch of concern for your safety. This has been a difficult experience for me, Mr. Peters," Toshiro said, stepping forward to look at the foot. "You'd better have a doctor take a look at that. Why are your shoes off?"

"Forget it," I said. "You were going to tell me about your difficult experience."

"Right," said Toshiro. "I'm afraid I'm what you would call a spy. Actually, it didn't work out quite that way. I mean I wasn't trained somewhere. My family does live in San Diego. We moved there from Tokyo about five years ago. I'm still a Japanese citizen. Japan is my country. American propaganda to the contrary, Japan is not totally at fault in what is going on. We are not totally innocent either. Well, to make this tale short, certain people from Japan contacted me because I am an aeronautical engineering student and asked me to take this job with Hughes and try to examine his papers if the opportunity arose, or if I could make it arise."

"And you failed," I guessed.

"Hell no," he smiled. "I got a full set of photographs the day before the party and left everything neat and clean. Then those Germans came in and botched up the whole thing. I was afraid the investigation would lead to me."

A figure appeared in the door with a gun. It was Paddy Whannel, the Scottish studio guard, who looked completely befuddled by what he saw—an unconscious woman on the floor, broken records all over the place, a guy with a bleeding foot and a young Japanese talking calmly.

"What the hell is this?" he said. "Peters, what's going on?"

"Paddy, my friend," I said. "I'm just beginning to find out. I suggest you lug the rather sturdy young lady out and tie her up. She murdered a couple of people. Then you might call the police and tell them to come here and pick up the more-than-suspect. I'll explain."

Whannel pointed his gun at Toshiro.

"Sure you'll be all right with him?" he said.

"No," I said, "but I'll take my chances."

Whannel holstered his gun and dragged Trudi away. In the hall, her heels made a double track in the NBC rug and we could hear him grunting.

"Doesn't leave me much time," said Toshiro.

"No," I said. "Your plan is to turn the photographs over to the Japanese government, the photographs of Hughes' plans for the bomber and the D-2 flying boat?

"Yes," said Toshiro, "but my government won't be able to do anything with them. I examined the plans carefully. Neither project is the slightest bit practical. The H-1 he designed back in '34 was a masterpiece. I've admired it for years, but the two projects he's planning now are the overweight products of an overworked mind."

"Then all this killing has been for nothing?" I said, wiping the bottom of my bare foot with Kleenex.

''It usually is,'' said Toshiro. ''I'll tell you what I'll do. I lifted Mrs. Gurstwald's camera from her glove compartment before I came in. It probably still has the undeveloped photographs she took of Hughes' plans. You can have it and give it back to Hughes. That way he's happy and thinks his plans are safe, my government is happy and no one else gets hurt.''

''And you?''

''I get the hell out of here, go back to my family and drive to Mexico tonight. Then tomorrow we get a flight back to Tokyo. In a few hours all hell is going to break loose in this country, and I don't want to be here. I've got the word that places have already been designated for interning Japanese Americans and Japanese nationals as soon as the war starts.''

''You're letting your imagination go too far,'' I said.

He took a small camera out of his pocket and handed it to me.

''You going to try to stop me?'' he said.

''I owe you my life,'' I said. ''I've got a soft head and a long memory. Have a good trip.''

I looked up and Toshiro was gone.

In five minutes, after soaking my leg in cold water in an NBC sink and being interrupted only once by the engineer, who had seen me through the studio window, I found Paddy Whannel and we waited for the police.

It was somewhere about two when my brother and Steve Seidman arrived. My watch said two-twenty. Even a stopped watch has to be right twice a day, someone once told me. Or maybe I read it on the wall of the YMCA toilet.

''They called me at home when they heard your name,''

Phil explained, leading me into an office Paddy Whannel provided. Seidman stayed outside. Phil needed a shave. The grey stubble on his chin made him look old and mean.

He closed the door behind us and said, "Explain."

I explained fast, weaving a tale mostly of truth. I told about Trudi, Martin Schell and Barton. I told him they had tried to steal Hughes' plans and failed. I didn't tell him about Toshiro. I suggested he check Trudi's gun and talk to her. I was sure she'd be willing to talk. He said Seidman was talking to her.

"So she killed the butler and Barton," Phil said perceptively. "Who killed the guy in Minck's dental chair?"

"A Nazi who can't speak English," I said. "A short guy with a lot of neck. Seidman and the FBI were with him at County Hospital yesterday."

Phil's angry look came on fast.

"How the hell did you know that?"

"I have a vast network of spies," I said, and he moved at me with clenched fists. "For God's sake," I yelled, "I'm handing you murderers and spies all wrapped up to give to the FBI, and you want to further cripple a crippled man. Where's your gratitude?"

He took my face in his big right hand, brought it close to his and then pushed me away. Then he held his hands together to keep them from doing something we would both regret.

"The guy in the hospital was named Kirst," said Phil. "He's dead. Got hit by a car. You wouldn't know anything about that, would you?"

"No," I said.

"Now, why did he strangle the Nazi in your office?"

"Double-cross," I said. "Wolfgang Schell wasn't supposed to kill me. He was supposed to find out how I fit in, but he got carried away and tried to kill me. Kirst tried to stop him, and they had a fight. He pummeled the hell out of Kirst. Some of the wounds on his body didn't come from that automobile accident."

"We know," Phil said suspiciously. "Go on."

"So, Kirst bled all over the place, got mad and strangled Schell in the dental chair."

Now if Phil didn't check blood types, or if the blood types of Kirst and the blood in Shelly's office matched, everything was fine.

"That is one hell of a story," Phil sighed.

"You think the FBI will buy it?" I said.

He shrugged.

"How much of it is true?" he asked in an almost friendly way.

"Most of it. Enough."

"In a way, I don't give a damn," he said. "Three Nazis and a drunken Air Force major. Is she a Nazi too?" He pointed to the door, clearly meaning Trudi.

"If you mean a German, yes. If you mean a Nazi, no."

"They're all Nazis," Phil said, simplifying the world like a good cop.

Seidman knocked and came in.

"Well?" said Phil.

"She's a talker," said Seidman. "Confessed to two murders, cried, pleaded. Said something about someone hitting her."

"I did," I said. "She was going to shoot me. I kicked the gun out of her hand."

''Night guard out there said something about a Japanese guy,'' said Seidman, looking at me. Phil looked at me.

''Chinese,'' I said. ''Here visiting a friend or something. Saw the mess and stuck his head in to see if he could help. I didn't get his name. He gave it. Loo or Chan or something like that.''

''Get out,'' said Phil. ''Fast before your ass falls off from all the lies. Get out, you shit.'' He raged and threw something in my general direction. It was an NBC ashtray. It almost hit Seidman.

I went out and hobbled down the hall as fast as my legs would carry me. I retrieved my shoes from the studio but couldn't get them on, so I hopped across the parking lot, afraid to step on the pebbles, and got into my car.

Driving to Mirador with a cracked windshield wasn't the easiest thing I've done, but with the help of three more of Dr. Parry's pills-for-all-ills, I made it by four in the morning.

The front door was answered by one of the two neatly dressed guards. He let me in and followed me up to Hughes' study. Hughes looked up from his drawings at me as if he had almost forgotten who he was. For some reason, he was wearing his fedora tilted back on his head.

''I'm alive,'' I said.

''That's good, really,'' said Hughes with something vaguely near enthusiasm. ''Did you find out if they stole any of my plans?''

''Don't you want to know who murdered three people?'' I asked.

''No,'' he said. ''The less I know, the less people can ask me.''

I pulled the small Leica out of my pocket and threw it to him. He caught it almost as well as Joe Dimaggio.

"What they had is in there," I said. "They never got to develop it. If you want to develop it, you can just to be sure I'm telling the truth."

"I will," he said emotionlessly.

I laughed. "You don't even know when you're insulting someone."

"I thought I was just being practical," he said. "I wasn't trying to insult you. You've done a good job, and you can be sure your bill will be paid in full."

"And that's it?"

Hughes had turned back to whatever he was working on.

"You were hired for a job. You were paid for a job. You did the job. I told you I appreciate professionalism."

I was tempted to tell him the plans in front of him were of no interest to Japan or probably anyone else, but it wasn't worth the effort, and I had more work to do, and miles to go.

The bruiser in the flannel suit let me out of the door, and I drove through the first rays of dawn over the ratty main street of Mirador, taking my last look at Hijo's, the bait shop, the police station and the car door in the middle of the street. I purposely cracked into the edge of the car door, sending it spinning toward the curb. It came to a screeching stop at the door of the police station. I had done my part to clean up Mirador in more ways than one.

I didn't admire the dawn through my cracked windshield as I squinted my way back to Los Angeles slowly.

It was a strange early morning Los Angeles I seldom saw, with no people on the street.

I stopped for breakfast at a we-never-close place. I still couldn't get my shoes on.

"What can I get you, Spirit of 76?" said the counter man, looking at my bandaged head and shoeless feet, which brought laughs to some early morning mailmen and a truck driver or two.

"You can get me a cannon for Christmas I can shove in your mouth," I said and sat at the counter. I didn't like what I was going to have to do, and I wasn't in the mood for jokes.

"Hey, I was just kidding," said the counterman, who looked like a recently converted alcoholic. "The boys can tell you I'm a kidder. Ain't I, boys?"

The boys agreed he was a kidder, but one of the boys scooted to a stool further from me.

"O.K., Red Skelton, get me a double bowl of Shredded Wheat with what you have passing for cream, and I'll dump my own sugar on it. And get me a coffee in something like a clean cup."

"You don't have to get sore, Mac," said the counterman, wiping his hands on his apron.

"You're forgiven," I said, making a sign like I saw a priest do once in a movie. One of the mailmen thought about laughing, but my mashed face, broken head and ridiculous foot changed his mind. I was really hell on a stool, I was.

I ate the Shredded Wheat and left the counterman a big tip. I'd make a good tale for him to tell the rest of the shift. It was nothing compared to what I could have told him.

I drove the Buick to Al's garage, but it was Sunday and Al wasn't there. I left it in the gas station for him with the keys under the front seat. He'd see the windshield and know what to do.

Then I limped to my office. The place was empty. It was Sunday. Even crooked lawyers and pornographers get a day off. I was feeling good and sorry for Toby Peters as I went slowly up the stairs carrying my shoes.

The new sign on the doorway was in gold letters.

Doctor Sheldon Minck, Dentist, D.D.S., S.D.
Painless Dentistry Practice Since 1916

Toby Peters
Investigator

I wasn't even "private" any more. The alcove had been cleaned up somewhat, and a new chart, this one showing the inside of a tooth, covered the bullet holes. Someone had cleaned the ashtrays.

Shelly's office even showed signs that there had been a halfhearted attempt to clean it up. I went to my office, found an envelope from Hughes with two days pay and called the phone company to find out it was almost eight in the morning. Then I called Basil Rathbone.

A woman answered and got him.

"Yes?" he said.

"It's me, Toby Peters," I said with a great yawn. Then I told him what had happened.

"I see," he said, when I had finished. "And now you have one more bit of business to take care of. Would you like my advice?"

"Go ahead," I said.

"Holmes often took justice into his own hands. It was rather a hubristic act, but he was a man of tremendous ego. While you may not fancy yourself such a man, this case may require other than simplistic action."

"I understand," I said, looking up at the baleful eyes of both my father, who had wanted me to be a lawyer, and my brother Phil, who wanted me to leave him alone, and Kaiser Wilhelm, who simply wanted me.

"Thanks for the help, Basil," I said.

"Glad of whatever assistance I could provide. I'd like to keep in touch."

"I'll do that," I said and we hung up after the good-byes.

My plan was to make some coffee and wait, but I couldn't get my feet and body out from behind the desk, so I pulled out my notebook and began to transfer my expenses for the case.

Bumpers, bribes, tremendous quantities of gas, parking, phone calls, dinners, windshields, doctor bills, brought the whole thing to $198.60. I had put in six full days. I decided not to count that morning. That made $288 in per diem rate, minus the $192 advance. That made another $96, which meant Howard Hughes owed me an additional $284.00. Considering what I had gone through, it didn't look like a hell of a lot, especially after paying for the office and car damage. Without another good job or two soon, I'd be hocking the coat I bought in Chicago.

I typed the bill neatly on some Nevers Trucking Company stationery, which had been given to me as a present by Nevers when his company went out of business after he went behind bars for five years for hijacking. I had done some work for his lawyer, leg work, but everything I found had made Nevers look worse. He had held no grudge and given me a stack of stationery.

Stumbling back into Shelly's office, I found a scalpel and brought it back to my office to sharpen a pencil, with which I crossed off the letterhead for Nevers, using the side of an envelope to keep the lines straight. Then, I neatly penciled in my name. So much for the professionalism Howard Hughes expected from me. I put the bill in an envelope, licked it and put a two-cent stamp in the corner.

The case was officially closed, but there was that one nagging unofficial thing to do.

I turned on the radio and listened to a Sunday morning preacher warn me about the wicked paths, the evil in the world and my own responsibility. I must have been really in shock. He actually seemed to make sense to me.

Listening got difficult. He yelled louder to keep me awake, and I vowed to remember his words, but my head went down, and some time between heaven and hell I was sleeping with my head on my arms.

I dreamed of yesterdays, baseball games, a dog running and a man who told me why I dreamed about Cincinnati. I wanted to remember what he said, so I could think about it when I woke up, but I was interrupted by an airplane that dove into a hangar and came out the other end.

Then I was standing in a dark hall, and someone was walking through the darkness toward me. It was a little kid, a boy. He stamped on my sore foot and tried to reach my head. He was very matter of fact and unemotional about it, and he was wearing a fedora like Howard Hughes. I covered my head with my hands and called for help from Koko the Clown.

He came bouncing in and jumped on my head to help protect me, but the little kid's punches went through Koko, landing on my wound.

I ran from the kid, still carrying Koko on my head, and hid in a closet. I could hear the kid coming closer. The closet was dark and someone was showing a movie on the wall. I tried to get to the projector to stop so it wouldn't attract the kid, but I couldn't get through the glass wall. Koko wouldn't get off my head, and footsteps were coming closer.

"For God's sake, help," I tried to say, but nothing came out. I was mute, my mouth dry.

I woke up and slipped off the chair. Someone was in the outer office. I thought I knew who it would be. I threw water on my face from the sink behind me and called out.

"What time. . ." I squealed and cleared my throat. "What time is it?"

"Almost noon," came the voice from the other room.

I moved around the desk and headed for the door and the person who had killed Wolfgang Schell in the dental chair.

CHAPTER THIRTEEN

I made some Ben-Hur coffee and realized that I had left the radio on. Music was coming through softly, and it sounded all right in the quiet building.

"You want some coffee?" I said.

He said yes, and I poured him a cup.

I started to sit in the dental chair and thought better of it. I sat on the stool. He sat in the dental chair.

"What happened to your foot and your head?" he asked, sipping his coffee.

"Everybody asks that one," I said.

"Under the circumstances, it's a natural question," he said.

"I'll tell you later," I said. "I told the police a now-dead Nazi named Kirst killed the guy in the dental chair." The coffee was awful, but I poured myself some more.

"They believed you?"

"They accepted it," I said.

"How did you know I did it?" he said gently.

"Lots of little things put together," I said. "Partly a

couple of words in blood about a 'child' and partly a comment by Basil Rathbone about the butler not doing it. It's funny,'' I said. ''The butler did do it.''

Jeremy Butler's huge mouth turned into a slight smile.

''Schell, the guy in the chair, saw your nephew, didn't he?'' I said. ''I remember your saying that night that your nephew was coming to see you. He must have been with you when you heard the noise. You came out in the hall and saw Schell about to shoot me. Right so far?''

''Yes,'' said Butler, finishing his coffee and warming his hands on the now-empty cup.

''Then, when he fired a couple at you and that didn't stop you, he backed into the chair and you got to him. He couldn't very well write your name in blood. He didn't know your name. The thing that struck him was the kid behind you so he wrote 'child' in blood, hoping his brother would put something together and get a bit of European revenge. How'm I doing?''

''Very well,'' said Butler.

''How badly did you get hit?'' I said.

He shrugged and lifted his shirt. A four-inch white bandage circled his stomach, holding a large patch of gauze held firm with adhesive tape. Butler's stomach wasn't as hard as it had been a couple of years back when he threw 300-pounders to the canvas with body slams, but it was all right.

''The wound wasn't bad,'' he said. ''I've had worse from old ladies' umbrellas after a wrestling match.''

''Glad to hear it.''

''What do we do now?'' asked Butler.

''Nothing,'' I said. ''You saved my life. What good

is it going to do to go to the cops? How's your nephew taking it?"

"Marco's a tough kid. Looks about ten but is thirteen. He hasn't started to grow yet. He thinks I'm a hero. He was too young to ever see me wrestle."

We had some more coffee and said nothing, just listened to the radio.

"I came here the last three days to see you and talk about it, Toby," he said. "But you weren't here."

"It worked out," I said.

We were quiet for a few minutes more.

"Thanks again, Jeremy," I said. The moment was turning awkward and I was ready for rest. He took my hand, which was lost in his, gave me a smile and left.

I turned off the radio and caught a cab home. It was Sunday. Gunther was making lunch in his room, and I joined him at his invitation. I told him the long tale and he listened attentively while he neatly buttered his bread. Gunther was wearing his suit, but he seemed to have nowhere to go.

We ate fish soup, quietly listening to the radio, and I felt calm and peaceful for the first time in months.

Gunther told me about his work for Brecht and his fear that the new translator, Bentley, would be getting it in the future. However, Brecht had steered him to a number of friends who were going to Gunther for more work translating Danish.

Our lunch was just about finished when we heard the phone ring, followed by Mrs. Plaut's loud voice beyond the door. Then came her familiar padding feet.

"Mr. Peelers?" she shouted at my door. "Mr. Peelers? Telephone."

I moved to the door as fast as I could and out of Gunther's room. I caught her still knocking and yelling at my door.

"I'm here, Mrs. Plaut," I said.

"You're not in your room," she said in her flowered robe, holding it together with a firm, wrinkled right hand to keep me from peeking.

"I know," I said.

"I thought you were in your room," she said.

"I'm clearly not," I said.

"What happened to your body?" she said, looking at me.

"I went four rounds in an exhibition with Joe Louis," I explained.

"I didn't know you were a boxer," she said in awe and new respect. "I thought you were a private exterminator."

"No," I said, "I'm a. . .forget it. Yes, I'm a boxer."

"You're homely enough," she pondered.

"Thank you. Is the phone call for me?"

"The phone call is for you."

I moved down the hall and left her mumbling toward the other direction.

"Peters," I said. "This is my day off. Call me in the office tomorrow. Late tomorrow. If I'm not there, leave a message."

"It's me, Shelly. Is that you Toby?"

"I just said it was me."

"The bill for fixing the office came to forty dollars. You still owe me. . . ."

"I'll pay you tomorrow. Why does everything have to end on details? Can't a man have the satisfaction of doing his job and just sitting back for a few days in peace and physical agony?"

"I know how you feel," Shelly sympathized. "When I pull a couple of impacted ones, I want to have a drink and take a few days to recover."

"You fill me with confidence, Shelly," I said. "I admire the new door."

"Thanks. Hey, there's a message for you. I left it near the autoclave or in it. I can't remember. Maybe on your door. It wasn't important."

"Then it can wait till tomorrow," I said. "Have a good Sunday, Shel."

"Just a nut who said he was Boris Karloff," Shelly chuckled. "Did a lousy imitation. Left a number. I answered him with my Peter Lorre."

"What did he say?" I asked.

"He said he had a problem. Something about a vampire or something. It was a dumb joke and a dumb imitation, believe me. 'Tell Mr. Peters it is urgent,' " Shelly said, imitating Boris Karloff. " 'Vampires, he said.' "

"I'll call him Monday, Shel. Goodbye."

I hung up. Boris Karloff and vampires. I went through the catalogue of characters who might pull a dumb joke like that and was on the sixth name when I gave up and wondered why a joker would actually leave a number to call. There was an outside chance that Boris Karloff had actually called me. I'd worry about it the next day. This was my day for resting bones and mending in the sun on the front porch while I listened to little girls jump rope to violent chants and racial slurs. It was a day to contemplate calling Carmen the waitress at Levy's and suggesting an outing in the park. It was a day to be a human being and not a private investigator.

I went back to Gunther's room to help with the dishes, but they were finished.

The music was playing and I fumbled in my pants pocket for a nickel to call Carmen. Maybe she could put together a picnic from Levy's for her and me and Gunther.

But such was not to be. The music on the radio stopped with a hum of static followed by the voice of an announcer.

"Ladies and gentlemen," he said. "We interrupt this program to bring you the following special announcement. The Japanese have just launched a massive air attack on Pearl Harbor in Hawaii. Although no official statement has come from the White House, this sneak attack is clearly an open act of war, and it is expected that President Roosevelt will, indeed, declare war on Japan immediately. We repeat. The Japanese have just. . ."

I turned off the radio. The pain in my head was back, and I changed my mind about what I was going to do with this Sunday. I was going to find a store open somewhere and buy presents for my brother's kids, Nate, David and the baby, Lucy, and I was going to spend the afternoon with them listening to Orson Welles and *Quick as a Flash* and the news if they wanted me. I was pretty sure they'd want me.